monsoon MADNESS

GAE RUSK

Granville Island Publishing
www.GranvilleIslandPublishing.com

National Library of Canada Cataloguing in Publication

Rusk, Gae, 1952-
Monsoon madness / Gae Rusk.

ISBN 1-894694-21-X

I. Title.
PS3618.U75M65 2004 813'.6 C2004-900157-4

Author's assistant: Laura Christine
Editing: Jean Lawrence
Copy editing: Arlene Prunkl
Cover and text design: Leon Phillips
Cover photograph: Thomas Kelly ©1986

Front and back covers: details from wall at Tusha Hiti (royal bath) at Sundari chowk, a tantric shrine and palace. Patan, Nepal. 17th century.

First Printing: January 2005

Granville Island Publishing
Suite 212 - 1656 Duranleau
Vancouver, BC • V6H 3S4
604-688-0320 • toll-free 1-877-688-0320
email: info@granvilleislandpublishing.com
www.granvilleislandpublishing.com

Printed in Hong Kong

Quotes from "Prometheus Bound," *Aeschylus II*, pp. 138-180.
Edited by David Grene and Richard Lattimore. Translated by
David Grene. Chicago: University of Chicago Press, 1956.

The carved panel on the front cover depicts the deity Vishnu and his
consort Laxmi in tantric form. Multiple limbs and heads on tantric
deities symbolize omnipotence and their ferocious appearance
mirrors man's when faced with his fate.
Medieval Patan kings came to worship, meditate and bathe at
Tusha Hiti, a Sundari chowk.

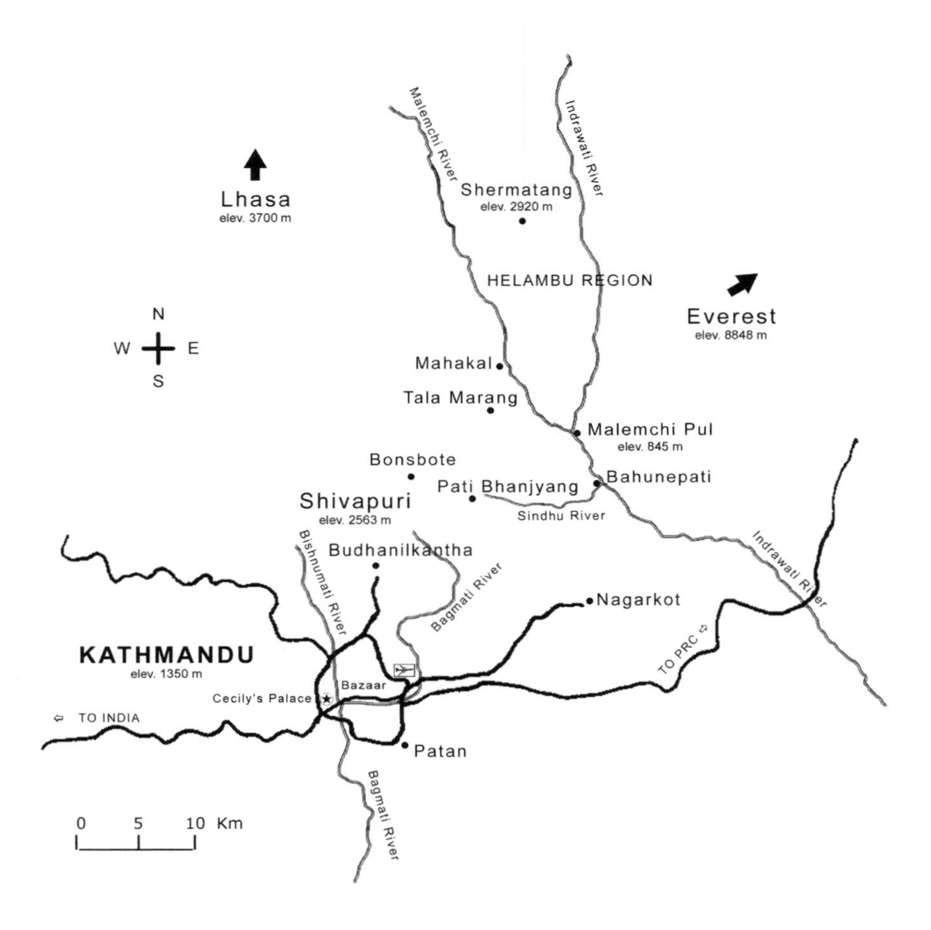
Lhasa
elev. 3700 m
Malemchi River
Indrawati River
Shermatang
elev. 2920 m
HELAMBU REGION
Everest
elev. 8848 m
N
W
E
S
Mahakal
Tala Marang
Malemchi Pul
elev. 845 m
Bonsbote
Pati Bhanjyang
Bahunepati
Shivapuri
elev. 2563 m
Sindhu River
Bishnumati River
Budhanilkantha
Bagmati River
Nagarkot
Indrawati River
KATHMANDU
elev. 1350 m
TO PRC
Bazaar
Cecily's Palace
TO INDIA
Patan
Bagmati River
0
5
10 Km

CONTENTS

PROLOGUE

OLD GODS, NEW TRICKS

Io:
"Zeus is stricken with lust for you;
he is afire to try the bed of love
with you: do not disdain him."

Prometheus:
"He was a God and sought to lie in love
with this girl who was mortal, and on
her he brought this curse of wandering ... "

THE OLD GODS ARE NOT NICE, and this is not a love story. It is too mythic to be a lovely, tidy tale of happy endings, although it just might lead to the ever after part. But what's this about the old gods?

Old gods were exaggerated personalities acting out extreme behavior. They were capable of astounding vengeance and such stunning sexuality that they often left mortals reeling for eternity.

But the sprawls of migration and mobility have displaced the old gods. Their temples are now well-managed ruins or buried under newer temples for younger gods. Their gardens and glades have been mapped out of existence by the latest hordes to pelt the landscape, forcing them to resettle wherever their believers chose.

When there are no more believers, which does happen, the old gods do not just disappear. Cut loose from the towline of religion, the old gods now travel solo. They frolic alone, solitary sightseers through space and time, mostly because gods don't play well with other gods.

So to Nepal, where Kathmandu is an exotic Parnassus and Everest an extreme Olympus. Nepal is a sanctuary for all these idle immortals. Like the multitude of birds crossing Nepal, they crisscross these jagged peaks because the ancient city is a beacon for gods, old and new, revered and forgotten, adored and scorned.

And when they get a mortal in their sights, bad things — merciless, lustful, malicious things — can happen. Fate is often toyed with. Injury is almost certain.

Ask Leda. Ask Danaë. Ask Daphne and Alcmene and Sylvia and Callisto. Ask Io.

So what of these ravished, ravaged women? These targets of deitic affection and heroic rape? Their fates were sealed long ago, recorded for all to know in art and literature as eternal consorts of the old gods. They now traverse those same rarified highways, more solitary sightseers for better and for worse and definitely for eternity.

The question is, in Nepal, where all gods fly in to claim their due, does any mortal stand a chance of survival?

Especially one like Cecily Havenshack, who is having a tantric tantrum deep in Kathmandu's old bazaar as the monsoon of 1978 settles over the mountains.

PART 1

CECILY BOUND

May, 1978

Io:
"...clearly you shall hear all you want
to know from me."

Kathmandu, Nepal

1

THE RAINS ARE LATE. Flies swarm around snorting pigs in the bed of the mighty Bagmati River, now reduced to a miserable, squalid trickle. In the heart of Kathmandu's bazaar, every third bare-assed toddler will die of a fly-borne disease unless monsoon soon makes its way to the parched valley.

On a western curve of Ring Road out past the Bagmati, a palace styled in the height of French Empire sprawls across an old Rana estate. With the Ranas' fortunes long ago passed into other hands, this estate is currently owned by a Brahman merchant living down in Bihar. He's made a bundle renting it to foreign diplomats who can afford to live the splendid life in Kathmandu Valley.

In a bedroom on the second floor, a mirror reflects French windows open to a view of Newar farmhouses scattering to the Himalayan foothills. The reflection is a haze of ocher and earth inside a gold-leafed frame fashioned in the complicated style favored by Kathmandu's francophiles.

This pastoral reflection is obscured when a woman leans forward to study herself. Oblivious to the view off her balcony, Cecily Havenshack leans closer and carefully plucks one hair from her left eyebrow. She leans back and frowns at the result. She fretfully shrugs slender shoulders rising bare from her black dress.

As the spouse of a US diplomat posted to Kathmandu, her biggest problem is anxiety about being left alone for so long. Fear of solitude has created profound distress about Stewart leaving for three months on a trip he claims isn't considered home leave. His wife isn't part of the deal and should just stay here in the valley, like a good spouse, ok?

Cecily bends to slip on narrow leather sandals, briefly revealing the exotic reflection of Kathmandu Valley behind her. Straightening and assessing her feet, she arches against thin leather soles. A black strap falls off her shoulder. As she catches and slowly pulls the strap back up, Cecily reflects on her miserable last few weeks. Her feelings are clearly mixed. Her eyes are lit by a private flame. The room darkens when long-overdue clouds begin to march across the valley, Cecily's mouth becoming a swollen bruise in the sudden gloom of the mirror.

Before leaving for three months, Stewart Havenshack tried to comfort Cecily during the hours between work and his social obligations. He insisted he had no choice but to go if they want a better posting, maybe Nairobi or Madrid. She should know by now that to get any promotion Stewart has to go that extra mile (in this case twelve thousand miles) and drink that extra cocktail, write those endless reports and make all these solo trips to DC and NYC and Brussels.

Cecily feels strongly that Stewart is acting too single-mindedly about his career and almost everything. Just last night, he lounged on the old Persian rug across the end of their bed and watched his wife wrap gifts for his family, half listening to her fret about small things. When Cecily was in the middle of imitating the cook hexing the gardener's wife that very morning, Stewart suddenly laughed uproariously, then told a joke he'd heard at work. She did not get the joke, but Stewart didn't notice.

It was after he stopped chuckling that Stewart glanced at Cecily, silent, sorting items on the Chinese carpet on the floor. He hesitated, breathed deeply once, then asked her a question. Little did she know, this question was to begin a sequence of events that would forever alter Cecily Havenshack.

"Hey, Cess?"

She was folding his underwear into perfect squares.

"Yes?"

Stewart cleared his throat uneasily, staring at Cecily's bowed head. He studied the coffered ceiling, finally asking, "What would make you hate me?"

Cecily looked up from the socks she was stuffing into a corner of his suitcase. She repeated uncertainly, "Make me hate you?"

"No, no, not really hate me, just pretend. You know, just pretend there was something I could do that would make you hate me."

She stuck a lone sock between wrapped gifts she'd purchased for his family and began pushing his boxers around. "That's stupid. Why are you asking this?"

He smiled mysteriously, reached over and pinched her nose, pretending to steal it. She went very still for one deep breath, then continued packing. She'd never told Stewart how much she disliked having her nose touched.

He leaned closer, put her nose back, his broad shoulders looming over her. "Say, for instance, I dye my hair blonde."

Through gritted teeth Cecily replied, "Bleach."

"Ok, ok! So? Bleached-blonde."

It was such a ludicrous thought that she giggled. "You'd look pretty silly, Stewart."

"But what if I did it anyway?"

She stared, incredulous. "Are you serious?"

He only shrugged, watching her closely as she jammed the rest of his underwear into a wad in the center of the suitcase.

"I don't know, Stewart! I can't imagine you doing something so juvenile!"

Staring at her thoughtfully, he asked, "So what if I bleached it darker, like black, blue-black?"

She frowned at him, then replied, "Dye!"

"What?"

"Dye! You dye hair black, bleach it blonde, Stewart."

His eyes narrowed as they always did when she corrected his grammar.

"Jesus H. Christ! So what if I dyed it black as coal?"

Cecily felt no satisfaction at needling her husband. What she felt was very close to panic, and she sputtered, "Really, Stewart! You'd have to be insane to do something that strange!"

She frowned at the suitcase, her voice suddenly quivering. "Wouldn't you?" and, "Why are you asking me this?"

He shifted uncomfortably. "Cess, honey, hey! I'm just trying to understand at what point you would, well, I don't know exactly what, but I guess, what it would take to make you pissed off enough to hate me."

She searched her husband's face and whispered, "What are you planning, Stewart?"

He opened his mouth to protest, but Cecily continued after swallowing carefully, "I mean, you could tell me in a better way if you're thinking about doing something horrible."

Her eyes filled with tears.

"Oh, Cess! Hey hey, don't cry, dodo!"

A high keening of Hindi radio wafted through the French doors and across the room. They could hear the washerwoman and the hexed gardener's wife talking out in the yard, and also the shriek of a Tata truck coming round Ring Road. Cecily's eyes dried and her hiccupping stopped. Stewart embraced her and gradually she grew a bit sleepy in the shelter of his arms. He murmured against her hair, "So what if I dyed my hair red?"

Incensed, Cecily pushed away from him, brushing curls from her eyes.

"What a stupid conversation!"

"Oh, come on! You know I'm not serious, Cecily!"

She clearly didn't believe him, sitting stiff and outraged, her face turned away. He twisted one of her errant curls around his finger.

"I mean, I am serious, but not really. This is hypothetical, Cess."

Cecily pouted. Stewart leaned over and touched his tongue to her throat. Her eyes widened as he reached her ear.

"Would you hate me if I got an earring?"

Edging away, Cecily considered her husband narrowly.

"I might."

He met her suspicion with a straight face for a few seconds, then he began to laugh. She reached over the suitcase and punched him hard, which led to arm wrestling on the floor among his bags. Then, eventually, she returned to the business of arranging way too much in one suitcase. Stewart leaned on an elbow to watch.

"What if I shaved my head?"

"Oh shut up!"

She didn't look up but her posture was wary, tense from making herself believe that he was just teasing her. Not his fault that she was so dismayed about being alone in the valley till the end of monsoon. Uneasily she contemplated the rigors of daily life in Kathmandu, the boiling and filtering of water, if there even was water, and the constant power failures and fuel shortages. She swallowed hard to keep from groaning just as Stewart interrupted these depressing thoughts.

"So? Ask me."

"Ask you what?"

"Ask me what you could do so I would hate you."

Cecily began to grow more than a little frightened.

"Why, for god's sake!"

"For curiosity's sake."

"Stewart, there's nothing I would do that would be that, that — silly!"

"No, come on. Think of something you could do. I mean, of course, something that wouldn't really happen."

He ran his hand up between her thighs so suddenly she grew dizzy. She bit her lip trying to concentrate, and the pain helped her focus above her waist. She considered his question. She turned a book of Himalayan photographs horizontal, placing it carefully among folded shirts. Finally she said, "Ok. Ok. So, what if I slept with another man?"

"Too common."

Nonchalantly, Stewart examined his fingernails. She persisted, "So? What if?"

He watched her turn the photo book back to its original position. She did not see his expression change as he struggled with telling or not telling her something, some mysterious and no doubt important information that he had and she didn't. Instead he said, oh so casually, "I think it would be ok with a friend."

She couldn't believe he'd said that. Cecily stared at this man she called husband. She felt like stuffing the socks in her hand down his throat, but Stewart quickly slid his hand up her leg again, finding that tender spot just behind her knee. He wasn't playing fair at all, she thought, when she could think again.

She blurted out, "Ok, what if I got a tattoo?"

Stewart sighed, his sarcasm gentle. "Cecily, honey, your imagination runs away with you."

She drew away from him, but he grabbed her from behind and was only half gentle as he held her to the floor.

Much later, Cecily had everything crammed into two suitcases, but they still wouldn't close, not even with Stewart sitting on them. She muttered a curse and began to rearrange the contents while he lounged on the floor beside her, his long legs bare and burnished gold by lamplight. He absently stroked her skin.

Because of their lovemaking and then two cognacs since he'd toppled her to the floor, she was enjoying a much needed moment of calm when Stewart said, "Well? You've had plenty of time to think about it."

Her eyes snapped wide open. He contemplated the cognac in his snifter, continuing, "So what could you possibly do that would make me hate you?"

She shouted, "Christ, Stewart! I don't know!"

She took a deep breath and asked, her voice carefully neutral, "Why is this so important?"

Stewart made no effort to reply. He smiled, his eyes beguiling, and Cecily considered her husband's pale beauty, his ingenuous air. She swallowed bewilderment, she forced back angry bile. Yes. Well. If Stewart wanted to play this sick little game, then play it they would. Studying her perfectly lacquered nails, Cecily groped for some heinous act.

"All right. Let's see. What if I committed a crime?"

He actually laughed. She eyed him with intense dislike, thinking furiously.

"Ok. What if I ran away with your boss?"

Stewart hooted, "That zero! Cecily, honey, you've got to be kidding!"

She cast about for something so bad he would shut up and go away and never come back. "Ok, you, what if I — what if I — what if I spent all our money!"

And she sat back on her heels, chin up, eyes glittering.

"I could do it, too! Like that!"

Stewart stood up and wrapped his robe tight around his waist, clearly unamused. "Not funny."

He added, "You better not;" emphasizing each word.

Cecily gaped, too astonished to respond in time to have any impact. Finally, she asked, "Why is that so much worse than anything else?"

He sullenly replied, "If you don't understand, there's no explanation simple enough."

"Oh come on, Stewart! Why is it worse for me to spend our money than sleep with someone else, or be a thief?"

No response. She leaned forward, truly curious. "Tell me!"

But it was clear that Stewart no longer found the game to his liking.

They did not sleep much that night, and as they made love in the morning before work, his last day in Kathmandu for ninety-two long ones, Cecily wept when Stewart came and went.

And now, sitting here at the old French mirror in her enormous bedroom in this Rana palace, she plucks another hair from her eyebrow, oblivious to the ancient valley pulsing all around. What could Stewart have meant with his mean little game?

Pushing back the ottoman, blocking the mirror again with a floating and settling of her black dress, Cecily admits to herself that she merely functioned at work all day, giving her students so much library time that they all went to sleep in the swelter of dry season's end. During lunch break she consoled herself with melted chocolate on dry toast and watched the fan circle overhead. She had vowed she would smile Stewart off, knowing now that really she will cry and will continue crying for three months.

Eyebrow plucked, skin perfumed and dressed in a frock the color of Western mourning, Cecily tries valiantly to make their last few minutes lighthearted.

"Don't you dare come back with a tattoo!"

Stewart turns away, turns back as if to say something. But whatever it is Cecily senses he wants to tell her, he doesn't, and instead he strides down the long drive and out the gate to find a taxi.

That very moment the rains begin with a thundering, dust-crunching deluge. She stands deafened and shivering under the porte cochère.

When Stewart doesn't return with a taxi for his two bulging suitcases, Cecily wrings her hands and steps from side to side. Finally she grabs an umbrella and runs down the long drive and out the gate and around the corner, to find Stewart all dry under an overhang. He's teasing the street kids by tossing coins in the air and catching them before the children have a chance.

Wet wind plasters black silk against her skin. Mud oozes into her Italian sandals. But all is forgotten when he looks up and smiles that wonderful lazy smile she already misses.

2

THE LAST WEEKS OF SCHOOL drag along under a low monsoon sky riding everyone like a tight hat. Each night Cecily tosses about trying to find deep sleep. No matter that the next day will go into a stall before lunch, she still ends up reading until 2:00 a.m., then drops into a brief and carbonated slumber, finally saying out loud after a night of refolding everything in her drawers, "Perhaps I am ill?"

So, on Wednesday at last bell, she catches the Kathmandu International School bus down to the bazaar to visit Dr. Jay Bahadur Shrestha, an Ayurvedic healer well known for his uncanny diagnoses and foul prescriptions. She squeezes in next to the silliest pair of first graders she hopes ever to meet, and they bump and sway together on their way to the bazaar.

Righting herself after stumbling off the school bus, she clutches her purse under one arm and grasps her Hong Kong golf umbrella as if arming herself. She believes she just might survive the traffic and avoid the excrement everywhere, but her true challenge is not to flinch as these wretched street children tug on her clothes and shout, "Bye-bye, memsahib" and "One rupee, memsahib." Cecily staggers when the last little beggar tries to hug her legs. She regains her balance, straightens her skirt and walks faster.

Weaving her way through the diseased humans who crowd the grounds outside *Bir* Hospital, she wonders if proximity will effect any cures. She successfully avoids eye contact with everyone except one young man, who is not ill unless his Levis are strangling him, and soon enters darker, calmer paths leading deep into the heart of Kathmandu's bazaar.

Ahead of her, a red *sari* vibrates as a Newar woman passes through shafts of light. Red dominates the very air in the oldest parts of the bazaar. Red bricks in buildings, red *tikas* on third eyes, red yarn plaited into long black braids. Red paste lavished upon a forest of reddened *lingam* and crimson *yoni*.

Herself a splash of fresh green linen, Cecily quickens her pace. She turns left into a dim canyon between ancient brick tenements. Only a few streaks of afternoon light slant down.

Unexpectedly, Cecily feels hair rise up the back of her neck and she falters, sensing someone — or something? — waiting in the shadows just ahead. Or maybe behind her?

She stops, paralyzed. What is it, a noise? A smell? And then, he or it is gone.

Pedestrians nudge her back. Holding her umbrella tighter, she walks forward, sweat beading her upper lip. A few more twists and turns and she will reach a tunnel that leads into Dr. Shrestha's courtyard. She runs this last stretch. Once there, she takes a moment to compose herself before ducking low into the tunnel. Upon making the error of breathing, she gags at a stench twelve centuries old.

After staggering out into a large, light-filled courtyard, she swallows carefully and grimaces; Dr. Shrestha will diagnose terminal halitosis. She hopes to god there isn't a long wait to see him today, but of course there is.

Sitting on a high-backed wooden chair (Irish, late nineteenth century, she decides), one of many scattered around the patio, Cecily pulls out Mauriac's *Second Thoughts* and opens it to page one. No, the first chapter begins on page nine. Is that significant? She closes the book and studies the people waiting to see Dr. Shrestha.

All the other foreigners look like residents of Freak Street off Dhurbar Square. She eyes two women (Danish? she wonders) sitting together, and she is mystified yet again by the outfits this type of world traveler wears in public. "Sick, sick, sick," Cecily mutters into her hand. She inspects the flattering line of her tailored skirt, reaching to pluck a loose thread from the hem.

Two patients exit Dr. Shrestha's ancient office door. Wearing punjab pants and a swinging vesty thing and not much else, the woman (Italian, she's pretty sure) floats with bare-armed, emaciated grace. Her companion (German? Austrian?) stumbles on the uneven steps and strikes his head on a low beam. Cecily raises *Second Thoughts* to hide her giggle.

Another foreign male (American? No, Australian. No no, wait, Russian? Hmmm. American?) who has been sitting behind Cecily, moves past her and ducks through the door into Dr. Shrestha's office. As he turns, his profile is visible for just a moment before the door swings shut, and she feels another chill surge up from her toes.

Flustered, she squirms on the hard chair. Noticing that her foot is twitching, she uncrosses and recrosses her knees and fans herself with *Second Thoughts.*

Her thoughts arrive at Stewart, the absent spouse. Cecily sees her husband accomplishing his time in DC in a way sure to get Madrid, which would be ok with her. Or at least Nairobi. They could like either assignment, they would do well at either assignment because they clearly have what it takes to do well anywhere. So why did he begin that incredibly stupid conversation the night before he left? Is it divorce he wants, after so many years of a marriage she has considered safely above average? Ridiculous! Ridiculous. He was simply teasing, he must have been teasing, he has always enjoyed teasing her even though she's asked him over and over not to.

She frowns and shifts on her chair, struggling to shake off her melancholy by focusing on the carved windows in the wall just across the courtyard. Soon, surely, it will be her turn? At that moment, Dr. Shrestha's door opens.

The man straightens from the low doorway. Towering above everyone else, he stares straight at Cecily.

She looks at his scuffed boots, up his long Levied legs, up to his thick black curls. She puzzles over his face and marvels at his magnificent nose.

He goes completely still, as if moving will scare her away. But Cecily drops her eyes at once. She uncrosses her legs, pulls at her skirt and sits up straighter.

He almost says something, but she refuses to look up, although she feels her flaming cheeks speaking for her loud and clear. She senses the man frowning under that incredible nose. He snorts and strides past her so close that air drifts across her skin and she shudders.

Unable to stop herself, Cecily swivels and watches him cross the courtyard. When he reaches the tunnel, he turns and eyes her again. She swings back around on the hard squeaky chair, then tries to calm the pounding of her blood with *Second Thoughts.*

3

THE LAST TEN DAYS of school have to be faced, but Cecily finds herself with no inspiration to teach. Keeping her students intelligently occupied takes too much effort for too little result.

These same bored and muttering students consider some of the other teachers their buddies, but not Mrs. Havenshack, who is so formal and gives way too much homework, then grades way too hard. None of them guess her strictness is because she has to grade them; therefore, she cannot be their friend. Cecily has never understood how other teachers can do both.

Principal Edna Balderwin has more than once admonished that she needs to be more open so the children will want to share their hopes, air their problems. Horrified at the thought of encouraging such confidences, Cecily reaches a point of not believing it has all reached such a point.

She is more than normally stressed out for reasons far beyond the strain of teaching — an unexpected houseguest has arrived and settled in, a most unwanted complication.

Then, in the pandemonium of the last week of school, Edna Balderwin, with her normal poor timing, schedules a conference with Cecily. To top this, Edna does not reveal that their supposedly private meeting has become a group conference, and Cecily arrives unprepared for the group.

Three parents sit in Edna Balderwin's office. Cecily stares without comprehension. Of the three, two glare back, and Cecily suddenly recognizes them all: they are the parents of the three kids closest to failing her classes. It crosses her mind that she makes herself unavailable to listen to their problems because they have so very many problems.

The British diplomat father eyes Cecily a bit warily. During that last winter they met a few times at official functions and did not have much to say to each other. She is struck with another thought: perhaps her predicament here is a result of all those cocktail parties where she'd been too shy to talk to anyone. She only went to them at all because Stewart made her go, and she generally ended up sitting in a corner eating too many hors d'oeuvres. Cecily can almost hear the British father thinking, If this woman is so aloof with me, does she even notice my child? Hampered by these thoughts, Cecily falls onto a chair, then tries not to cower.

After an eternity of Edna Balderwin eliciting complaints about her from these parents, a pall falls over the group, partly because Cecily has not opened her mouth once the whole time. She still sits mute in a now ridiculously long silence. The British father coughs, rises and says he really must be going. The Korean mother stands at once, clearly relieved that someone has finally made a move for the door. The American mother rises a bit later, more reluctant, obviously hoping to draw blood before leaving. Mrs. Balderwin frustrates Cecily's attempt to follow the group out the door and guides her back to a chair.

"Now, I'm really very sorry I didn't make the purpose of this meeting clear to you before you walked in here. I thought I had."

Edna pauses, waiting in vain for Cecily to say it's ok. Clearing her throat, the principal continues, "The reason for all this, Cecily, is not to condemn your academic program; I don't want you to change that, believe me. Yet, I've observed in your teaching, a certain, let us call it a degree of coldness when dealing with your students."

When, wonders Cecily resentfully, did you last come into my classroom to observe anything.

"Now, I'm not saying that I don't think you care about them as people, but you're so short with them when they're not perfect that you scare them. Certainly, they need to be made aware of their behavior when it's harmful to others, but they also need to be listened to with a smile for their hurts."

At this point Cecily feels tears coming, and she cannot believe she is going to cry in front of this woman whom she truly despises. Even if Edna Balderwin is maybe even slightly right, she still despises her. But, while Cecily teeters there on the brink of a storm of tears and remorse, Edna Balderwin makes a tactical error.

"To prove a point, I ran a little survey among some of the students."

Cecily's mouth, open to admit any and all guilt, slowly closes.

"Now, I asked only four questions, and I didn't ask for names, just for classes. The results unfortunately support what I've been trying to point out to you all year."

Cecily's eyes narrow and begin to dry. Mrs. Balderwin perches half-glasses on her nose, peering down at a sheet on her desk.

"I asked, One, which class do you like the most? Two, which class do you like the least? Three, in which class do you feel you have the best relationship with the teacher? Four, in which class do you feel you have the worst relationship with the teacher?"

Mrs. Balderwin eyes her over the rim of her glasses. "Now, I want you to remember I mentioned no names. And still, the answers to numbers two and four, well, on number four alone seventeen out of twenty-five seniors named American Lit as the class in which they have their worst relationship with any teacher."

Cecily feels all the liquid in her body rush to her eyes. She twists her hands in an effort to control this flood while Balderwin continues to watch her closely.

Then and there she knows she will never forgive Edna Balderwin for making her cry. Never ever, and if Stewart weren't already long gone to DC, she would go home and tell him she was quitting as of this moment. But he is twelve thousand miles and three months away, and her contract at the International School has two semesters to go.

She fights for control of her turbulent thoughts. She composes her voice with great effort. "Mrs. Balderwin, I disagree with you, and I will never agree with you, because I won't be, become a, a, a mother confessor for them just because —"

This is as far as she gets. Edna firmly ushers her out of the room, the principal as usual having the final say. "Just trying to help you and the school. Just doing my job."

It isn't until late that evening that Cecily thinks of all the really important questions left out of Balderwin's little survey. Like, "In which class did you learn the most?" Or, "For what part of your year-end tests were you best prepared?" Or, "Who taught you a skill you will use your entire life?"

However, by late evening she is far too preoccupied with her uninvited houseguest, Stewart's old friend Joel Carnune, to go find Edna Balderwin and quit her job.

4

ON THE FRIDAY BEFORE the last week of school, six days before her disastrous conference with Edna Balderwin, Cecily arrives home just as the phone rings. Tired, but actually more relaxed because she's finally sleeping better, she throws her books on a table and picks up the heavy, decades-old phone.

It is Stewart's college roommate, Joel Carnune, calling from the airport. He's just finished a job in Delhi and decided this very morning to see Kathmandu before returning to Manhattan, and since Stew has invited him to visit how many times, well, Joel thought, "So what do you think? May I stay with you for a couple of weeks while I play tourist?"

Cecily bites off a fingernail while she listens. She had no idea Joel was in India, in Delhi no less! And if Stewart knew before he left he did not inform her. She wants to cry out, No! Go away! But what she actually says is, "Of course, don't be absurd! Of course you will stay here. Don't be silly!"

He is clearly very pleased. This makes her anxious for some unclear reason, but it isn't because Stewart isn't here to do the guided tours, the shopping, the watching out that Joel doesn't drink tap water or eat salad in restaurants or destroy his health in a dozen other ways. It isn't because she's given half the palace staff extended vacations, and now, with Joel's arrival, those still on duty will have more work than anticipated.

More likely, Joel's arrival is upsetting because, like a first class fool, she once upon a time fell headlong in love with him. It happened during those last months before the wedding when she briefly moved in with Stewart and Joel.

Granted, the morning she walked up the aisle and saw Stewart waiting for her, all thoughts of Joel (a yellow rosebud in his lapel, his green eyes intent upon her) were put aside. She is, by now, long over Joel Carnune.

When she mentions Stewart's recent departure, Joel doesn't sound the least bit disappointed. He doesn't even sound that surprised. Suppressing another pitter of anxiety, Cecily says to hang out on the curb, she will be there in twenty minutes to pick him up. Then she sits, phone in hand, at the hall table, until the receiver turns grouchy.

Dazed, Cecily stands and trails through several rooms to the master suite, pacing through giant squares of light spilling through the French doors. Why in the world has Joel picked this particular time to visit, when he must know monsoon covers the mountains so there's nothing to see? Following this thought to no conclusion, she smoothes gold-flecked curls down her neck, the gesture a familiar friend though it never seems to calm her curls.

She stares into the recesses of an enormous closet with garments hanging two rows deep. As pleased as she was with them up to this morning, now none will do. She reaches in, pulls out a skirt and holds it up to a row of blouses before dropping it to the floor. She stares helplessly into a closet bursting with all the wrong clothes.

A glance at the clock, yikes! Joel has already been waiting fifteen minutes since his call. Her stomach spasms, hands clench as she figures out that a taxi to the airport takes no less than fifteen minutes, which does not include the time it takes to find a taxi. Why, oh why, did she promise to be there so quickly?

Flipping through her wardrobe racks, Cecily rejects each item as unsuitable for wearing to the airport to pick up Joel Carnune. Turning and dashing down several long corridors to a far guest room, she wrenches open a closet full of garments saved for special occasions. The shantung? One of the Thai silks? Maybe that orchid blue? She's never worn it, so it might give her a sense of, of what? Of something she clearly is not and never will be.

Upon fastening the belt and running all the way back to her full-length mirror, she remembers why the orchid blue has never been worn. She tears it off and lets it drift to the floor to land upon the colorful pile of rejects.

Glancing at the clock, Cecily calculates twenty-seven minutes have passed. She should be there already! She stands undecided, dithering, cursing Joel and her tailor.

Suddenly, she feels too grimy to think about putting on clean clothes. She veers into her bathroom, deciding to cool down before she has a full panic attack. She'll surely have more success choosing an outfit after a quick bath.

But of course, there is no water. The toilet won't even flush. Already undressed, Cecily grabs a towel and tries to wrap it around her slight body, but it is more of a hand towel. Holding it as close as possible, glad the palace stands so deserted today, she jogs to the sunroom's open French windows to shout for the *mali*.

"Krishna! Krishna!"

No answer from the garden.

"Krishna!"

Going from window to window, Cecily finally remembers that the *mali* is off till Sunday morning. Great. She shouts louder for the *chokidar*, "Shiva! Shiva? Where are you?"

He, as usual, is late to the gate. She yells in frustration, "Somebody! Yoohoo?"

Her voice settles over the estate under the weight of monsoon drizzle. No answer from any direction. She wonders uneasily if she sent everyone on vacation. It's possible. Frustrated, overwhelmed by the need to bathe, she decides she will just go out and turn on the blasted pump herself.

Avoiding the clock on her nightstand, she skids into her bedroom. She sure hopes Joel is not as impatient with her as he used to be. Cringing at that thought, Cecily grabs a pair of ancient jeans and a crumpled T-shirt from the dirty clothes hamper, struggling into them on her way to the door.

Luckily her driveway is long. She uses that distance to zip her Levis and pull down the shirt as she runs barefoot past the rose garden, past the hedge maze, past row after row of enormous vegetables on both sides of the drive, and through the small copse of fragrant trees planted by an English bride of a long dead Rana. She aims for the pumphouse just inside the main gate at the same time her *chokidar* arrives on his bicycle.

She veers aside at the last moment, yelling, "*Paani china!*" without slowing down. With memsahib charging at him like the rhinos in his Terai village and yelling at him, Shiva backs out the gate faster than he rolled in.

Meanwhile, Cecily hops the low wall to the tank, and struggles to slide the concrete block aside to see that there actually is water in the cistern, for she burnt the pump dry last winter much to everyone's dismay. Seeing water below, she sprints over the low wall to the pump switch. Pausing only long enough to make sure the blasted thing begins, hitting her thighs with her fists while the machinery chokes to life, she whirls and dashes back up the drive.

Part way to the house, she turns her ankle on a crumbling brick and falls to one knee in the mud. Hell and Hades! But she is up and off again, inside and down all the long halls, finally skidding to a stop in the palatial bathroom.

When she finally wrenches on the tap, her reward is the gasp and suck of dry pipes. She turns it off, counts to ten and turns it on again, but no water gushes forth.

She can't believe it. Still panting, her heart pounding, she makes herself sit on the edge of the bathtub and look out one of the floor-to-ceiling windows. She rolls her sweat-soaked shoulders and breathes deeply, concentrating on the view. The shutters frame verdant fields stretching away to three-thousand-meter foothills that border the west end of the valley. A few distant farmers are limned by sidelight as they bend over rice shoots, because the setting sun is casting a golden pelt across the scene. It brings to mind a Vermeer she saw once in — Sunset! Oh, my god!

Moaning in frustration, Cecily reaches for her brush and begins pulling at her hair, brush and stroke, head back, head forward. She opens her eyes. Focusing upon the medicine cabinet, she spies her husband's forgotten deodorant. This evokes a vision of Stewart in DC, listening attentively to older diplomats, shaking hands with well-dressed alpha females.

She bends and again turns the tap: a gurgle, nothing else, and she finally faces the fact that there is no tap water and there will be no tap water anytime soon. Another shudder from the pipes galvanizes her to action, and she races once again to the sunroom windows.

"Shiva! Shiva!"

Damn it, where is he? There!

"Shiva! Taxi!"

He waves and trots out the gate. Cecily heads to the kitchen. There, she hefts one of the kettles onto her hip, then staggers to the bathroom where she pours some of her precious boiled and filtered drinking water into the basin before she realizes it isn't plugged. Struggling to hold the kettle with one arm, she gropes for the stopper. Where is it? Twisting her neck till it pops and her teeth clench in pain, she finally spies the damned plug lying on the rim of the tub.

After sliding the drumlike kettle to the floor, plugging the drain, then hefting the kettle once again to the sink, Cecily washes quickly, sliding a wet cloth under her T-shirt. She locates a toothbrush but no toothpaste. She runs the faithful hairbrush through her curls once more for luck, then hurries down a long hall, down curved stairs and across the foyer to the loud horn of a taxi coming up the drive.

She pauses at a gilded mirror hanging above a Regency table. Her eyes reflect limpid green as one lone tear rolls down the side of her nose.

"Stewie baby, why aren't you here?" she whispers. The taxi blares another summons.

"I'm coming!"

Coming coming, coming coming.

5

THE RIDE TO THE AIRPORT is upsetting for the taxi driver. First memsahib says, "Hurry, I'm late!"

So he does. Then she cries out, "Slow down!"

So he does. Then memsahib yells, "Not this slow, damn you!"

This curse is punctuated by a shriek when he misses by at least a meter that old woman crossing the road. The driver shakes his head in pity. Too bad such a young memsahib will die when her head explodes.

Cecily looks down at her lap, up at the patched ceiling, everywhere but forward. She attempts yoga breathing. The fifteen minutes to the airport stretch to twenty-five because of rush hour traffic. By now, Joel has been waiting for seventy-two minutes. As the cab at last careens toward the curb outside the terminal, she spots him sitting on his bags, staring moodily at the ground. The set of his broad shoulders is ominous.

"*Yahaa roknos.* Stop!"

The taxi jerks to a standstill, pitching Cecily forward. Joel does not look around. Staring at his profile, she reaches inside her bag to retrieve her sunglasses and shoves them on with trembling fingers. She fumbles open the door and stands. Holding firmly to the door, she croaks, "Joel?"

He swivels round, he stands, and Cecily's chest tightens. Lord, he's even more gorgeous! She lifts an unsteady hand and wiggles her fingers. Joel smiles and strides to her, kisses her cheek, hugs her shoulders and murmurs, "Cecily Havenshack!"

He steps back, touching her lightly as if testing to see if she's real. Joel's gaze, still eerily the same shade of green as her own watchful eyes, sweeps down to her feet and back up again. There is amusement in his voice. "The same! Charming."

She wrenches her eyes from his and uneasily looks down to find she's still wearing her oldest jeans, one knee muddy, and a tight French T-shirt that reads "Beau Geste" across her chest. Stewart would pretend not to know her.

Cecily regards Joel with growing alarm. Lord, he really is as beautiful as any man could ever be. And his eyes, well, Stewart used to tease them about having the same green eyes. Several times Stewart said his best girl and his best friend must be mirrors of the same soul and other such nonsense, until she told him in a voice thick with emotion to just give them a break, ok? Stewart gave her the silent treatment for several days, and she now recalls feeling sick with the tension of it all.

Joel steps around the taxi door and moves close, touching her chin and bending a light kiss upon her lips. Cecily's knees wobble. Then, recalling where they are, she gasps and stammers, "Joel! I'm so g-glad to see you, I mean that, I was late, you see, because — "

She stops and starts over, striving for more composure. "And you've just committed your first faux pas in Nepal. Two of them, actually."

He is clearly amused, chuckling, "Kissing my best friend's wife, and — ? Hmm?"

The last thing she wants to do is make him laugh at her. Joel never bothered to hide that he found Cecily so very amusing and so very cute, but a child really, after all. She winces at the ugly memory of what she overheard Joel tell Stewart late one night when they both thought her upstairs already asleep. She can still hear him drawl that he, Joel, enjoyed watching Cecily's precious little tush anytime day or night, but she was so, well, acted so young, didn't she. Such a blank slate, hmm?

What Joel and Stewart hadn't realized was that Cecily was not upstairs all tucked in. She was standing on one bare foot on the cold linoleum kitchen floor, pouring herself a glass of milk, and she began to tremble with mortification when she overheard Joel's comment. She spilled the milk then made it worse by trying to mop it up with her flannel nightgown and not make any noise at all. This frantic, silent flurry caused her to miss hearing Stewart's reply — his defense of Cecily.

Now at Kathmandu International Airport, she remembers with regret how she knelt on the kitchen floor in pure misery. Afraid of going back upstairs, that they might hear her, that they might catch her in a milk-soaked nightgown! Standing behind the swinging door in the kitchen, cold, barefoot, biting her bottom lip, until she felt it safe to slip upstairs and back into bed unheard.

It was that very night that Cecily unhappily admitted to herself that she was besotted with Joel Carnune. She was appalled at the intensity of her feelings and almost had a nervous breakdown trying to appear normal, but somehow they'd all continued to live together until two weeks before the wedding, when Cecily flew home to her family. She wept bitterly the whole way.

She saw Joel again only twice before moving abroad. The morning she walked up the aisle, Joel was standing at Stewart's side and she could almost see through him. Then, after returning from their honeymoon and settling into a small apartment in NYC, Joel came into town on business and spent the night with them. Joel watched her cute little tush all that night and the next morning, but he said nothing about Cecily's cool greeting, nor did he comment when she didn't respond as usual to his teasing. He did leave sooner than planned, and they hadn't seen him again in the months before going abroad, nor in the years since.

Laughter snaps her back to the present. Joel is amused that he's struck her dumb, and she is dismayed to find herself still as tongue-tied as she was after that night of cowering behind the kitchen door all those years ago. Even worse, Joel finds her unchanged: the same darling little Cecily, only older. He frowns.

"You're a bit thin, Cecily."

She looks down. Her misery is renewed at the sight of her outfit, and she shrugs awkwardly.

"Oh. Well, I've had a few parasites since we moved here. Everyone who comes here gets them."

The taxi takes off, pitching them back against the seat and into each other. She shoves Joel off and scrambles to her window. He voices concern that she even looks rather frail.

"Really? I feel fine. Fine!"

She swallows, controlling the panic in her voice, adding, "I'm quite active."

And I'm very stupid, she thinks, blushing rosily. He reaches for her hand, lacing her fingers in his.

"What were my two faux pas back there? Kissing you?"

"Yes, kissing me. I mean, not just kissing me, but kissing. In general."

He laughs and lifts her left hand and brushes it with his lips, murmuring, "What a deprived culture."

She tugs her fingers free, laughing hollowly.

"There you go again, the other mistake! You just kissed my left hand, which the locals use in place of toilet paper."

He laughs. Cecily has a moment of clarity; maybe she can get by if she becomes the entertaining nincompoop he knew back then.

Thus several kilometers pass and she does not flinch more than twice at the driver's erratic maneuvers. She remembers that she hasn't told him where to go, so he is merrily flooring it through the chaos. Where to go? Home? Lord, no! Not yet, anyway. Braving a brief look out the window, she observes no lull in rush hour. The rickshaws, water buffalo, bicycles, Tata trucks, mopeds and cars, all forming a warp for the pedestrians' weft, create a heaving vibrancy that makes her head swim. She gulps, thinks, then turns to Joel, asking, "Are you hungry? Do you like Japanese food?"

From contemplating the scenery, Joel looks over.

"Well, sure. But in Kathmandu?"

"Oh, you'd be surprised what can be found in Kathmandu."

After making this fairly stupid comment, Cecily huddles closer to her door. What possessed her to tell Joel he could stay two weeks? Joel continues watching her as she directs the driver to the only sushi bar in the Himalayas. The taxi surges sideways through a wall of bicycles.

Instead of observing the landmarks she tentatively identifies, Joel sits turned to Cecily. She finds his scrutiny stressful, although at one time she would have traded anything, possibly even Stewart, to be the object of Joel's attention. Now all he does is remind her of that sodden, miserable night she stood hiding behind the kitchen door.

After the taxi lurches to a stop in front of the restaurant, they remove themselves and the luggage. Joel fumbles for his wallet, but Cecily quickly shoves a wad of wrinkled rupees at the driver. They haul Joel's bags past the bye-byeing urchins and troop up a flight of creaking, narrow stairs and into a Japanese dining room filled with Nepali waiters. At Cecily's request, they are seated in one of the alcoves where the tables are so low they have to stick their feet into a well underneath. Cecily ends up facing the wall while Joel gets a view of her and the restaurant. The menus have to be held high to the dim light, and Cecily hides behind hers until the waiter arrives.

"Tea? Sake?"

"Both, I think. Mixed tempura. And miso soup. Joel?"

He asks her for a recommendation, and she answers, serious, "Anything hot. No raw sushi or cold anything if you like your good health."

"Oh yeah? So, guess I'll have the same."

Cecily instructs the waiter to bring tea before the meal, though she knows darn well he'll bring it whenever he likes. Joel pulls out a packet of *Galois* and offers her one but she declines, then fidgets while he studies her through smoke.

He leans forward across the low table to touch her hand. His proximity too much to bear, she leaps to her feet before she can think. Joel's irritation is evident, and Cecily stutters, "Excuse m-me, I-I'll be right back."

Joel blows smoke and watches her back up like a spooked doe. When he replies with remote courtesy, "Of course," she has no choice but to step out of the alcove and bend to slip on her shoes.

When she straightens and turns, brushing away curls that halo her face, Cecily looks up to lock gazes with that black-eyed man, the one she saw at Dr. Shrestha's. The tall, dark-skinned man with that marvelous nose. He is seated at a table between her and the only door leading to the toilet.

Tempted to leap backwards, she stands too still too long and Joel asks, "What's wrong?" She has to go forward despite having to pass so near this scary man with knowing eyes.

The man chews his food and watches her wary approach without once blinking. Ok. She can stand being stared at. She can stare back too, if only his eyes would remain on hers instead of moving down her neck, her shoulders, her — He's doing it again! How dare he!

When his eyes reach her chest, he suddenly laughs with his mouth full, showing Cecily a bunch of mushed up sushi. She is disgusted. She sneers and her lip curls, but when he keeps on laughing she uneasily looks down at her T-shirt, reading "Beau Geste" upside down. Looking up to find him still helpless with amusement, she stalks, chin up, past his table to the door leading out behind the kitchen. Almost there, she trips on a sandal strap she hasn't bothered to buckle and hits the door at a tilt. It flies open and she plunges into the dark passage beyond.

After catching her balance, Cecily tiptoes around puddles of murk illuminated by a red bulb high up on a swaying cord. She is furious: why that, that pubic hair! Showing her his mucked up food like a stupid kid!

When she shoves open the door to the dim and dank loo, one blue light floating overhead, she sees the floor is flooded. The concrete slopes so effluvium can drain around an elevated squat toilet, but clearly something is wrong. She has seen far worse, so breathing shallowly and praying for olfactory fatigue, she holds the door open with her hip, bends to roll up her Levis, tiptoes around the torpid, oily pond and finally leaps to the toilet's tiny atoll. Straddling it, and pulling up her Levis up from the ankles and down from the waist, she squats the best she can.

Because she is still shaking in rage at that cow turd out there in the restaurant, Cecily loses her concentration and ends up peeing down one ankle into her sandal. Jerking, she falls sideways, one hand sinking down through the fouled water to a floor sliming downhill.

"Oh Christ! Christ, Zeus, Athena and Thor!"

As she struggles to right herself and keep her Levis dry, hot fat tears squeeze out and trail down her cheeks. She stands and fumble-zips her pants, sniffling and wet-faced. She clumsily washes her hands over and over at the rusted sink. Ineffectively pushing at curls heavy on her forehead, Cecily feels like hell has reached up to baptize her.

This feeling is confirmed when she opens the door and a cloud of kitchen steam rolls over her so she can't see anything and has to feel her way back to the restaurant door. She splashes through all the puddles. Once inside the door, she marches stiff-backed to the alcove. She can feel that horrible stranger's eyes hot upon her back as she slips off her wet sandals.

Joel does not inquire why she looks so damp and flustered. After they eat an almost silent meal, he merely says, "You're probably wondering why I didn't let you know ahead of time I was coming out here."

She nods, still unable to speak. Joel continues blowing smoke at the ceiling, not meeting her eyes.

"Actually, I knew I was coming to India several months ago. My office needed someone for fieldwork and chose me, mainly because I'd never been east of Rome and would be able to see things with a fresh eye, so here I am."

Leaning forward to grind out his cigarette, Joel waits for her to speak. She strangles out, "Uh, you work with ...?"

"Food Aid International."

"Oh. In Delhi?"

"Calcutta, Bihar, east side of India. Sri Lanka, Bangladesh. Being here is on my own time."

He smiles his brilliant smile. Then, he asks questions about life in Kathmandu and what she's been doing to fill her time. No, he didn't know she was teaching at the International School, and for so long, too. Stewart hadn't mentioned it in any of his Christmas letters. This is a piece of information that dampens Cecily's remaining spirits. She gulps her sake and orders more.

When the tea arrives with the bill, Cecily quickly pays. Joel tries to grab it away, then leaves his hand on hers, causing her to look up into his emerald eyes. She yet again feels a surge of old misery from that night when she knelt shivering in the kitchen. Shaking off his hand, Cecily stands. Joel scrambles to grab his suitcases and follows her out of the restaurant, past the clamoring urchins and beggars and down the street.

"Cecily!"

She doesn't slow down or look back.

"Cecily, Cecily, wait a sec! Hey!"

Catching up, he grabs her arm and turns her around.

"Cecily, I must tell you something."

She knows she doesn't want to hear it and shakes her head vehemently, but Joel yells in her face, "I knew that Stewart would be gone."

Her eyes widen. He steps closer, looming, confiding, "I saw Stew in Delhi at a party a few weeks ago. He was bumped off his British Air flight, didn't you know? Well, anyway, we just ran into each other at this cocktail party and he told me he would be in DC the entire summer. And you were here, alone."

Cecily is speechless, and he continues more intimately, "When I found out he wouldn't be in Kathmandu with you, I, well, the next day I went down and bought a ticket up here."

He hesitates, then asks, "You aren't angry, are you?"

She shakes her head. Anger is not her predominant emotion at the moment, because her anger has already been spent on that black-eyed, hatchet-nosed cretin back in the Japanese restaurant. What she feels about Joel's revelation is simple astonishment.

Still, long years have passed and an older and wiser Cecily does not readily believe this confession. They stand in the dark among street children and rickshaws, the odd sounds and pungent smells of night-time Kathmandu a vivid setting for their private drama.

"I've always felt strongly about you, Cecily."

No answer to that. She knows better.

"I felt when we were living together that, well, that if it wasn't for Stewart being my best friend I'd want you to be mine."

He pauses to observe the impact of this. He is disconcerted by her impassivity.

"I've wanted you for years, Cecily, and finding out you were alone in Kathmandu seemed too incredible an opportunity to ignore."

He steps so close only Cecily's purse remains a barrier between them.

"I just hope I haven't alienated you by being up front about this."

Cecily keeps her expressive eyes lowered.

"Cecily?"

She doesn't believe a word of it. But she does not let Joel Carnune know that she knows what she knows. She steps back.

They continue walking for a ways, then catch a rickshaw. On their ride through the outskirts of town toward the palace, Cecily retrieves some of her composure. Harmoniums and candlelight set a poetic stage for the ride home.

Long after their arrival Joel is still exclaiming in wonder that the Havenshacks actually do live in a palace and he hadn't believed Stewart one bit. Cecily gives him his towels and a bathroom glass and explains the water situation for both drinking and bathing, adjusts his mosquito net and runs through a muddled and inaccurate listing of the household staff and her own work schedule. They part for the night without further overtures from Joel, though his smile lingers around her like that of some dratted cat.

6

SO, ON THE LAST THURSDAY of the school year Cecily tidies her desk, closes her classroom door and heads into the group encounter with Edna Balderwin and her three unhappy parents. Blissfully unprepared for the horror of this meeting, she passes the cafeteria, the lower-grade classrooms and the library, and she counts the days since Joel's arrival, coming up with six.

Though not quite as busy as she pretends to Joel, Cecily really does have a lot of work wrapping up the school year: exams to write on Sunday, personal errands to run on Monday, final essays to grade on Tuesday, and parties to attend each evening.

At these giddy end-of-school-year festivities, she abandons Joel to the more aggressive expats. The first night this happens, he goes along good-naturedly, but after the second evening, when Cecily quietly vanishes, he becomes a touch irritated.

By Tuesday, the fourth day of Joel's visit, Cecily feels the weight of his displeasure. She grumpily drinks too much and ends up standing alone in the darkest corner. Eventually she looks up from the fascinating pattern in the Persian carpet to find Joel eyeing her sternly from across the well-appointed room. She ducks her face, curls hide her eyes. Joel comes to a decision. He eases away from a group of foreign aid people who've been abroad too long, moves steadily through the crowd, grabs a moderately tipsy Cecily above one elbow and murmurs that perhaps they should call it a night.

Resentful and relieved, she smiles goofily all the way out. She's not so inebriated that she doesn't understand the hostess's smirky wink in the foyer. She turns away too quickly and runs straight into Joel. He holds her upright.

Though Cecily well knows that a taxi is hard to find this late at night in this part of Kathmandu, she forgot when dressing and slipped on heels that will not do well in the dark on rutted paths all the way to the nearest hotel. Immediately she trips and would have fallen flat except Joel catches her.

"Oh! Oh. Uh, thanks."

Within moments she stumbles again. He slips his arm around her waist.

"I've got you."

"I know!" is her annoyed response.

Joel looks down at Cecily's bare shoulder where her shawl has slipped off. Concentrating on her balance makes her unaware of his interest, which is lucky for her because walking is hard enough already. They continue for some time without speaking. Harmonium *ragas* resonate across the river. The spicy aroma of someone's late dinner reminds Cecily she never ate tonight. Joel's arm around her waist feels so tight that she grows uncomfortably warm. They turn a corner and she shouts, "Taxi!" with relief.

Home again, they crunch up the endless, pitch black drive after scaling the ancient brick wall because the modern metal gate is locked and Shiva is nowhere to be found. Even Shiva, her stalwart gate guard, has abandoned his post this monsoon. Inside the palace Cecily hurries away, touching lights as she goes, but Joel follows close on her heels.

He observes her flushed appearance with great interest. He says in a carefully neutral voice, "Thank you for all this entertainment, Cecily. I should have told you sooner, I know."

She replies over her shoulder, surprised into honesty, "You really like those people?"

He hesitates, his face shadowed. "Well, not particularly." He shrugs, "They're all right, I guess."

Cecily is embarrassed. "You should have said something."

"You're so good at avoiding me, I've had no opportunity."

She bends to plug in a lamp, pretending Joel didn't say that. He continues, "Cecily, you've been keeping me at arm's length since I arrived."

She succeeds in inserting the stubborn plug, but when she straightens and turns, Joel is only centimeters away.

"Cecily, Cecily."

He touches her nose with one finger, and she freezes, struggling valiantly not to slap his hand. Mistaking her mood, Joel moves even closer. His hands slide to her neck and she gasps. His lips catch hers lightly, briefly. He asks, "What, please tell me, have I done that so annoys you, sweet Cess?"

She blinks. He continues, mock-serious, "You remember who I am, don't you?"

Boy, does she. Cecily gulps, unable to say what she really wants to say, and instead chokes out, "It's just — I've got something on my mind, that's all."

She forces herself to step back. He does not touch her again that night but calmly considers her disjointed and inadequate reasons for her odd behavior as she backs out of the room.

The next morning, Wednesday, the fifth day of his visit, Joel does not get up to have breakfast with her. Cecily spends a despondent day at school, distant and sharp with her students. Halfway through her first class she is already depleted. What makes it all more difficult is that tonight is her turn to host an end-of-year event honoring the School's Nepali staff. As the day progresses, it becomes more and more unimaginable to her that the evening ahead holds anything but purgatory.

7

"MRS. CECILY, WHERE DO YOU want the champagne bucket?"

"Put it on the mahogany sideboard — that old carved thing in the small library, ok? And Preema, have someone keep candles lit in each room, I don't want anyone lost when we get a blackout." Cecily adds over her shoulder, "Hurricanes, Preema. Use the hurricane chimneys."

Preema is the only palace employee Cecily knows for sure will understand her instructions. Preema always knows what she wants done, extraordinarily so at times. If only Preema's grandmother, the palace's housekeeper, could get along with the head gardener's wife, and if only Cook wasn't so jealous of Preema being Cecily's confidante.

There is but half an hour before the first guests arrive, and Cecily has not even bathed. After an interminable Wednesday faculty meeting during which she and the other teachers squirmed and rolled their eyes, Edna Balderwin finally rambled to a halt before a clearly hostile audience. Cecily rushed home and threw herself into correcting all the party preparations executed by her eccentric staff.

A curious change has occurred in her house guest since last night. Joel smiles at her frenzy, laughs at her denunciations of Edna Balderwin and agrees with her distracted complaints about expat life in general. He pulls her down onto the old leather couch in the sunroom and, half in jest, makes her chant nonsense and take deep breaths.

Cecily is wary of this about-face in Joel's attitude, although his jokes do make her feel slightly better. She looks at her watch. Yikes! Twenty minutes to go, and she still has to bathe and dress, plus there's so much left to be done. Joel laughs and pulls her up from the low couch.

"You go take a bath."

"But, Joel!"

"You stink, Cecily."

She squeaks indignantly. He laughs and propels her into her bedroom and closes the door in her face.

Watching water fill the tub, a small miracle, she clenches her eyes shut and prays that things will be ok tonight. Maybe she won't have to hide in the kitchen. Maybe there'll be no need for liquor to find a semblance of calm. Perhaps she'll even eat a real meal tonight instead of forking food around her plate. She steps into the bath and stretches out and closes her eyes. As she floats there, she tries to convince herself that anxiety is self-indulgent.

Later, rubbing sandalwood oil across her smooth, brown belly, then fastening the strapless dress around under her arms, Cecily makes her spine relax knot by knot. She tries to see the situation from Joel's point of view. Maybe she's been unnecessarily hard on him; she's almost certainly spoiled his visit to Kathmandu by holding against him something she overheard him say years and years ago.

She hears people passing in the courtyard below and hurries her grooming. About to exit her bedroom, she is caught once again by her reflection in the huge mirror and realizes she hasn't untangled her hair since morning. Rummaging through toiletries without locating comb or brush, she simply runs her fingers through the wayward curls and gathers this glorious mess into a knot lying heavy on her neck. There. She closes her eyes, opens them wide and smiles at herself.

She never notices the red edge of a magnificent sunset slanting across the valley and filling the mirror behind her own reflection, though she does briefly pause and consider how flattering the light is tonight.

The party is all squeeze and hubbub. Hours pass, everyone grows giggly, in particular the guests smoking Thai sticks in the rose garden off the music room. Steam and clatter fill the kitchen as Cook flings food onto huge platters, which are then rushed to one of the groaning buffet tables Cecily has centerpieced in the rooms open to her guests.

During all this, she sees little of Joel. He is always on the opposite side of a room while she moves among the guests. She shrugs and widens her smile, admitting she deserves this.

Later, she escapes to her bedroom with Anna, her favorite colleague at school and her only real friend in Kathmandu. Anna makes herself comfy by arranging her long legs across the royal-sized, luxurious bed, while Cecily reclines at the other end and balances a glass of wine on her stomach and expresses relief at there being but two more days of school.

They drift for a moment, listening to party noises made distant by long halls and thick walls. Then Anna asks, "Are you sleeping with Joel?"

Cecily shoots up, forgetting the wineglass on her stomach. It overturns in her lap. Anna chuckles in her husky way when Cecily squeaks, "No! I'm not!"

Anna rescues the glass while Cecily stands and holds her dress up to keep from soaking the bed. With her head down and her back half-turned, Cecily resentfully adds, "Joel's an old friend of Stewart's. An old roommate."

"I know, I know! I'm sorry!"

Cecily frowns as her friend continues to be amused. She morosely examines her ruined outfit, "At least it was white wine. Do I smell?"

Anna sniffs, then waves her long, polished fingers before her face, "Yes, but you can change, hon. This is your room."

Cecily mutters ungraciously, "Yeah, but trust good old Edna to ask why in front of ten people."

She opens the nearest closet to find something to wear, shaking her curls out of her eyes as they escape the slipping bun. Anna leans back and idly picks at the knots of the patchwork quilt, watching Cecily closely.

"Did I startle you so much, then? About Joel?"

"Oh. Well, you know," Cecily hesitates and pulls out another long dress, her forehead wrinkled. "Joel is Stewart's best friend. And, if you recall, I am married to Stewart."

She frowns again at her two hundred outfits. Anna regards her thoughtfully.

"So? Why should that stop you from doing what you want when he abandons you?"

"Stewart didn't abandon me, Anna. He just went to DC for some training."

"And didn't invite you along, as he could easily have done. As he should have done."

Cecily tugs at the dress and considers this claim. It is true that Stewart just assumed she would stay here in Kathmandu, but it's also true she never questioned being left behind. She shakes her head to clear it of these unwanted thoughts, saying decisively, "Even if I did have an affair, I wouldn't have it with Stew's best friend. That wouldn't be right."

She slides a caftan of lemon dupioni silk over her shoulders. Then she turns to her friend, continuing, "Would you?"

Anna stares at the ceiling, smiling, still fingering the texture of the quilt.

"Have an affair? Probably. I mean, yes, I would, if it was no one anyone knew. The perfect stranger."

Anna's eyes refocus. She drops her gaze, adding, "And if he were interesting enough in other ways. And yes, definitely if Jimmy went back home and deliberately left me behind when he could easily have asked me to go with him, if only to be polite."

Cecily occupies herself by soaking up wine on the floor with the wet dress. These last words disturb her. Anna continues, "How long, exactly, will Stewart be in DC?"

Cecily rubs harder, more flustered than she cares for the other woman to know. She answers resentfully, "Twelve more weeks."

"Oh?"

Cecily's soft lips tighten. Really! Even if Anna is her best friend! A sound from the door interrupts them.

"Cecily? Is Cecily here? Hey, Cess, the Balderwins are almost out the door, I thought you'd want to know."

Joel stands in the doorway and smiles lazily at Anna, who stretches her legs and is all languor across the bed. Cecily stands with an awkward lurch, saying too loudly, "Of course! Mustn't miss that!"

She neither looks at Anna as she leaves nor answers the quizzical smile Joel gives her when he stops her at the door and retrieves from her cold hands her sopping wet dress.

8

THEN IT IS THURSDAY, the sixth day of Joel's visit, the day after the party, the day that Edna Balderwin, three parents and Cecily discuss her relationship with her students.

Cecily wants to scream at them that of course she is distant with their kids, anyone who knows them would do well to keep distant from such unmitigated brats. She is distant with Mrs. Balderwin because she cannot stand her, distant with Joel because she can't say what will occur if she isn't, and distant with Stewart because he's in DC, damn him. However, none of this is said aloud because, at the sight of the group in Edna Balderwin's office, Cecily's heart tries to exit through her throat, then sits trapped on her vocal cords the whole time.

Later she flees school holding back a typhoon of tears. Fearing Joel will see her crying, she keeps the tears damned up all the way home. Discovering he's still out comes too late, her angst has solidified. It sinks to the reef of grief that's been building through more years than she can remember.

For over an hour, she lies on her bed staring at the ceiling with a tissue gripped in her hand, hurting deep and sharp behind her eyes. When Joel returns at dusk, he sends Preema to tell Cecily he's back. Cajoled by her *didi*, she staggers to the bathroom to wash her face and bare her teeth in the mirror. She tells herself sternly not to reveal her troubles to Joel, not to spoil the rest of his visit.

"Hello, me darlin'!" calls Joel, when she walks into the library at the end of the west wing. Then he catches sight of her face and his words echo around the large room.

"Did you have a nice," Cecily swallows loudly, the words struggling up her throat, "time? Sightseeing?"

Their green eyes meet, hers slide away.

"Uhmmm. Saw a few temples, did some shopping for the folks. All right if I get a drink?" He indicates the liquor cart. She twists her wedding ring around and around and finally stammers, "I could, I mean, I'd like one, please."

He turns away, avoiding her eyes, giving her time to recover.

"Sure, Cecily, hon. Hey, why don't you sit down? Relax and all those good things you're supposed to do when you come home from the mines?"

Ice clinks. Cecily squeezes the Kleenex, cementing it to her palm and croaking, "Send the staff home."

"Excuse me?"

"Please, send everyone home! Tell them something, anything, I don't care! I don't want them here!" She sobs brokenly, "I don't want anyone here!"

The tears flow free at last. She bows her head. Crying makes her green eyes small and her small nose red, her usually soft body tight as a kettledrum. She blows into the pulp of tissue in her hand while Joel goes through the palace announcing early dismissal for the staff. The house quickly empties, an uneasy silence settling over the grounds. Meanwhile in the library, Cecily cries for all she's worth.

"Cecily, hon, come on over here. Sit down, come on now."

He leads her to the couch where she continues her grief. In a pool of lamplight, he holds her face to his shoulder, his chest, his lap, his chest again, nuzzling her curls. Finally, he slips off the couch, leaving her depleted and crumpled on the upholstery. He retrieves her drink and makes her swallow it quickly like water. Then he makes her another. She chokes part of it down.

"I'm all right now."

Her reassurance ends with a hiccup. He continues to stroke the back of her neck. She touches fingers to one temple and leans away from him, saying in a thin voice, "It was something to do with school, I just reached my limit about school."

He removes the glass from her trembling hand and begins rubbing her fingers and palms, then her arms that are clenched so tight they hurt as much as her head. A drawn-in breath aches on her teeth, and she shudders.

It is hard to concentrate on anything, the drinks making her dizzy and his hands confusing her. Is that his hand on her breast? She shakes her head in an effort to clear it, but she opens her eyes to find Joel only centimeters away. She opens her mouth to find his pressing upon hers, his body pressing upon hers till they tilt back and roll off the low couch and onto the Tibetan rug Stewart gave her just last Christmas. She makes a feeble protest, but can't get any words out with his mouth on hers. His weight on her body seems the only anchor she has to keep from swirling away.

It is some time before his kisses provide enough adrenaline to clear her mind so she can figure out that she doesn't want Joel to come to her, after all those wistful years, just because she's cried in his lap. It's too much like pity. Like comforting a child. Oh yes, it is just like comforting a child, patting Cecily's cute little tush.

Her eyes, after inordinate effort, stay open. The feel of his mouth and his hands and the anticipation of him inside her is more, much much more than she ever imagined, but she orders her hands to push him off anyway. They barely obey. Just enough to catch Joel's attention.

He growls, "Cecily!"

"Joel, nononononononono!"

Is that hysteria she hears? She pauses in amazement at her own voice.

Instead of rolling away and letting her up as she assumed he would, Joel grabs her hands and rolls back on top of her, forcing her still with his weight, silencing her with his lips. It works for quite a while, but the scratchy wool rug irritates Cecily's skin made tender by the pounding of her blood, and she pushes at him with all her strength.

"Why are you pushing me away, Cess?"

"Because."

Joel thinks that's very funny.

"Because, because, I don't want to."

He stops laughing, then one hand leaves her leg and follows the line of her chest to her chin. He says, "I'm using my right hand now."

He moves quickly, his other thumb suddenly up inside her panties. She is so aroused that her pudendum throbs and seeks its own pleasure. He asks again, "Because why, Cecily?"

She stares into his green eyes which continue so very like her own. He repeats his question while his hand does something magical around her labia. The lower half of her body pulses open, while from the waist up she struggles to her elbows in protest. Held immobile by the pressure of his hand between her legs, she does not answer until his eyes move so close to hers they appear to cross. She squirms backwards.

She gasps, "Because I'm not ready!"

Joel frowns. She blushes, continuing, "I don't mean I'm not ready, I mean I'm not, well, ready. Enough. Ready enough," she fumbles to a halt.

Joel laughs again, loudly. "Cecily Cecily, I love you! You know why I love you?"

She wonders that he can more than why he does.

"Because you're so unpredictably funny."

She stiffens. He continues chuckling. She finally asks, "Like a child? A ten-year-old, maybe?"

He tilts his head, puzzled, his gaze unwavering, but he does not answer and instead swivels his hips into hers. She takes a deep and shuddering breath, holding herself together with enormous effort.

"Joel, as you have most likely noticed, I'm not exactly averse to having, let us say, a brief affair with you."

She would never admit, among other things, how often in her life she has thought of it.

"But I am not, well, not prepared, for lack of a better word. I'm not ready for all the problems that come with an affair with anyone." Taking another deep breath, she adds, "But especially with you."

She stops looking into his eyes and stares at his strong hands where they rest below her waist. If he tries again, she won't stop him. Won't even try.

However, after a long silence that neither is inclined to break, Joel sits up pulling her with him and lets Cecily go as if releasing a small bird, his gesture wide and open.

9

THAT NIGHT CECILY LIES EXHAUSTED but never quite asleep. Sudden gusts of wind tickle her nerves but do not appear to move the gauze curtains. A soft knocking at the bedroom door slowly penetrates her half-awake nightmare. She grabs the covers and sits up, wide awake.

"Y-yes? Who is it?"

"It's Joel."

"Y-yes?"

He clears his throat, "I have something to tell you."

She pulls sheets to her throat. "What?"

"May I open the door? Please?"

Oh no. But she says, "Y-yes," then peers anxiously through the mosquito net at the silhouette in the doorway. She clutches the sheets tight.

"Cecily, I have to tell you something, I can't sleep if I don't. I — and before I do, I must tell you I've decided to leave tomorrow. I think I better, if I can get on a flight."

She also hopes he goes. But what she says is, "Joel! Don't leave because of tonight."

There is a singular lack of conviction in her plea. Joel shrugs impatiently.

"That's just it, Cecily, you don't know what happened tonight, you don't even know." He continues angrily, "That's what I have to tell you, goddamnit!"

This time she doesn't encourage him to continue. She probably doesn't want to hear what he has to tell her.

"I told you I saw Stewart in Delhi. Well, I didn't see him, exactly, and it didn't happen quite that way. I mean, Stewart heard from someone we both know that I was coming over this way, and he called me in New York. I wasn't yet in India, you see."

She is now sure she doesn't want to hear this story, but he ignores her protests.

"So we talked awhile, and then Stewart told me you'd be here all summer and, uh, and why didn't I go see you and, well, if I could, you see, would I," Joel swallows loudly, "would I sleep with you."

Cecily is too astonished to speak, but Joel raises his hand as if she has tried to stop him.

"Now, don't go blaming Stewart. I mean, don't think bad about him, Cecily, please don't. He did it, I mean he asked me to do it because he's concerned about you."

She repeats, "Concerned? Concerned?"

"He said you needed it."

She nearly shrieks, "He said *what?*"

Joel's distress is apparent by jerky movements in the doorway. "Please don't be angry or hurt or anything! Stewart asked me to do this because he loves you and wants you to have a good, uh, I mean a safe, uh, experience."

By now she is fuming. "But he wants to control it if I do? He wants to monitor it, does he?"

He steamrolls ahead as if she hasn't spoken. "Because you were, admit it, you were damn green when you two married, Cecily, and not what one could call, well, worldly to any degree. Even I could see that."

You're the asshole who pointed it out! She silently rages, furious that she can't get the words up from her heart and out of her mouth. She tries again; nothing comes out except an extended wheeze.

"So, he asked me to come see you while I was over here, and if it happened, it happened."

He sighs, "Well, it didn't."

Another anxious movement in the doorway.

"And I'm the one who's sorry, Cecily."

Cecily chokes out, "Joel, I don't want to hear any more!"

But he plows on, "I'm sorry it didn't happen because I thought it would be a lark, a friendly-type lark, you see. I always thought you'd be fun to sleep with. But, hell, I don't know! It's more than that now, because you're more than that now. You're more than just cute and fun like you used to be."

"Joel, please!"

"Not that I'm criticizing you, ok? It's just, well, Cecily, you've become kind of depressing to be around."

The room is silent after this last piece of wisdom. Joel strangles out, "I'm sorry! That was inexcusable." He sounds wretched. "I want you to know that I want you right now like I'd want any complicated, good-looking woman, and that makes all this not so innocent like I thought it would be, not at all."

He shakes his head, amazed at his own thought process. "I'm actually glad you turned me down. Because at first I was just going to do an old friend a favor by screwing his wife. But now, with you so different, I wouldn't have been doing Stewart a favor at all."

He swallows then confesses, "I would have made him a cuckold." He takes an unsteady breath, continuing, "And glad to do it!"

His words fly around her bedroom and perch maliciously on a bedpost and observe her reaction to this form of honesty. After what seems a long time, she says in a very small voice, "Go away, Joel."

"Cecily, please! I'm so sorry, I put it badly, I know."

"You put it quite well, I think, Joel. But I really don't want to hear any more. If there is any more?"

"I'm so sorry!"

His obvious distress causes her to reassure him in a strained little voice, "No, no, it's not that, it's just that I'm so tired, and, well, so tired."

Stepping back into the hall, he waits for her to say something else, but she clutches her sheets in silence. He sighs, "Ok, Cecily. I'll go quietly."

The next evening she sees him off to the airport, exactly one week from his arrival. Cecily feels inexplicably sad at their strained farewell.

Later, standing outside where tarmac meets fence, she clutches chain link. After Joel Carnune's plane passes the southern foothills, Cecily says with teeth-clenched precision to the back of Air Nepal, "I hate you now, Stewart. I hate you now."

PART II

LIMBO

June, 1978

Prometheus

"If anything of this is still obscure
or difficult ask me again and learn
clearly: I have more leisure than I wish."

10

MONSOON WEEPS INTO THE VALLEY. As her long holiday begins, Cecily makes only desultory attempts at movement. She does not even bother to collect her mail at Stewart's office. She feels September — Stewart's return, a new school year — will be soon enough to seek the company of others, so it isn't till the third week of holiday that she ventures out.

By now, the valley outside Kathmandu proper is a quilt of viridian fields defined by muddy dikes. Wood trim on rosy brick glistens with dry season dust washed away. Even the bazaar has renewed vigor.

One of Cecily's Newar colleagues has an endless supply of bazaar tales. Especially intriguing are stories about the Ranas, the valley's ruling family in the nineteenth century, who had porters carry things French up and over the Himalayan foothills to their vast estates in isolated Kathmandu Valley. The Ranas built regally. Their architecture stands even now as a unique blend of palace and pagoda, and the Havenshacks' leased estate is a good example of this Franco-centric style.

On her walks to and from the bazaar, she pokes her nose into obscure little temples and does some shopping at the smaller vendors. She realizes for the first time how many courtyards sit hidden inside the buildings leaning shoulder-to-shoulder along each alley. Typically, six full floors are stacked inside fifteen vertical meters, all creating a complex squalor as wonderful as it is appalling.

According to her Newar colleagues, up to very recent times no one wanted to live on a street wide enough that a carriage could roll through, because more than one noble ruler was known to snatch comely commoners from their very doorways. A victim's family might never know where she spent the rest of her life. She might as well be dead, a constant threat, anyway, if she fell into disfavor or was poisoned by the competition.

So went the stories. Intriguing. Possible. The bazaar actually is a puzzle, and most streets remain winding canyons. Doors the size of windows lurk half underground, a testament to the city's antiquity. To this day, Newar wedding processions are held after dark, a tradition dating from a time when the beauty of a bride or youth of the groom might attract royalty's amoral eye.

Cecily wants to believe these stories and not just because they explain the old bazaar. She doesn't quite believe it all because the contemporary Ranas she knows are so normal. They worry about things like soil erosion and interest rates, and it's unimaginable their grandfathers abducted virgins off these very cobblestones.

Kathmandu continues to engage her. When there is a break in monsoon showers, a walk through the bazaar provokes her senses without affecting her solitude. At night, her pile of lusty-gusty paperbacks is no match for a dream of virile prince and virgin maiden, and also one of virgin prince and virile maid. The dreams always evaporate before happy endings are realized, so she awakens restless and with a contrary appetite.

She pays closer attention to the careening traffic as she pedals her bicycle up through the bazaar for a swim at the club, or hikes to one of the English language libraries, or window shops down New Road.

One day she buys eleven pieces of imported fabric and takes them to her tailor. She surprises herself by choosing filmy georgettes and flowered silks instead of her usual neutral linens, but decides to go with it. Stewart will just wither up and die when he finds out she's spent so much money on new clothes.

As Cecily rolls by the turgid Bagmati at last filled with water, she says aloud, "Wither away, Stewie."

11

ON MONDAY MORNING OF THE 5TH WEEK of monsoon, Cook reminds Cecily-memsahib that it's payday. When memsahib sits down at an ornate Victorian desk in the smallest of her three libraries and counts out wages for Cook and two assistants, a housekeeper and three maids, one laundress, one gatekeeper and four gardeners, she finds herself five thousand rupees short. Recounting the pile of rupees, Cecily still comes up short by five grand. She pokes through each niche and cranny of the huge Victorian desk with no success.

In a mild panic, she counts once more with the same result: not enough rupees to pay her staff. Where's all her cash? She tries to think without hyperventilating. Let's see, some went for that dinner with Anna at Boris's new restaurant. And a few, what, maybe three lunches at the club, a few, maybe two, by the pool. Oh yes, that hammered-copper bowl she'd found up in Patan. Anything else? Oh yes. There was that hideous erotic carving Stewart bought just before he left; it's supposed to be centuries old and how her foolish husband plans to get it out of Nepal she doesn't want to know. She'd forgotten that he raided her monsoon cash to pay for it the day before he left. However, even counting that monstrosity, two thousand rupees remain unaccounted for.

For a single second, Cecily wonders if one of her staff took the money. That idea is quickly dismissed; it is too frightening a thought. She is determined to account for the missing rupees if she only thinks about it long enough. Of course, no matter what, she has to pay her staff today. This means cashing traveler's checks, which she hates to do because Stewart is such a fiend about exchange rates. She sighs. There is no choice, one simply has to pay one's employees.

So, at 9:15 Monday morning of the fifth week of monsoon, Cecily bicycles to the bazaar, pretending she's enjoying the ride when truthfully she's now so broke she can't possibly afford a taxi. Her bicycling leaves much to be desired, probably because she's so afraid of falling over. She knows from experience how injury, if not death, brushes by every few meters. Rules of the road are nonexistent. Trucks up from India shriek like banshees as they roll down into the valley. And signal to make a turn? Why? Everyone needs a little mystery in their lives. As for brakes, well, maybe on a cliff.

Today, after one narrow escape when a Tata truck barrels down on her off the Raj Path and she swerves into a hefty matron in a silk *sari* to avoid death, Cecily feels she might pass out. Then she runs over a pile of melons. While their owner yells at her a crowd gathers round to take sides. It costs twenty rupees to get the melon vendor calmed down, and the crowd is still milling when she awkwardly rolls away.

Gamely she speeds up and enters heavier traffic. A taxi swerves around the next corner, missing her by centimeters. She grips the handlebars, gasps, steadies herself. A rickshaw careens around the same corner, just missing her back tire, its bell clanging as an afterthought. Now seriously shaken, she wobbles deeper into the bazaar.

Her reward upon reaching the bank is not great, aside from still being alive. A sign states the door opens at ten. Locking her bike to a lamp pole takes a minute, leaving twenty-nine more to pass in the already stifling monsoon morning. She leans against the bank's closed door to wait, glad there is still some shade on this side of New Road.

And it would have been a good place to wait and watch New Road come alive on a Monday morning, except that her least favorite beggar in the whole bazaar shows up — the one who paints his very advanced elephantitis a virulent shade of purple. He knows from past experience that this particular memsahib gives in very quickly, and he closes in with his begging voice at high pitch. Cecily hastily pushes away from the bank's closed door and scurries back up New Road.

The charm of the rest of the bazaar is not to be found here. New Road offers manufactured goods from China, Tokyo, Hong Kong, the USA and Europe that lure shoppers up from India. Local jewel merchants line up trays of raw gems from Sri Lanka and Burma. Cecily stands pressed against one window, entranced by a star ruby rolling loose on a tray. Behind her, trucks and taxis nudge through the pedestrians, their fumes compromising air just washed clean by the early morning downpour.

She looks back at the bank and sighs. The beggar, plague take him, has stationed himself beside her bicycle. She trudges on down the block idly window shopping, it being too warm and humid to just stand still. She fights a desire to enter the shops and keeps walking away from the bank toward the next intersection, where she plans to cross New Road and meander back down the other side.

When she reaches the Suiting Room Cloth Shop, Cecily stops quite still. She suddenly remembers where those missing rupees went: the elusive two thousand rupees were spent on eleven lengths of the most exquisite cloth now at her tailor's, and she can't even remember very clearly what is being made. Taking a deep breath, choking on exhaust fumes, Cecily trudges on in a mood as foul as the air.

Half an hour later she sits on a hard chair, one of several in an uncomfortable line that wraps around the bank's small office. She arrived back from her walk to find the area free of beggars, and she stood first in line waiting for the door to open, but when it did, everyone rushed in and somehow she became ninth in line. She sits now eight chairs from the *topied* bank official and his *saried* assistant. She swears silently at pushy Euro-trash scumbags and smoothes a puckered seam of her tailored riding skirt. She still feels good about its crisp, camel lines.

The air grows thicker as they wait. An unpleasant odor wafts by. She fans her face with her book and tries not to stare, but really! With the outfits most of these budget travelers wear, what else can a normal person do but stare, mouth agape.

Finally Number One leaves and they all shift a seat closer. Number Two begins exchanging a pile of traveler's checks. Cecily eyes the six others ahead of her with increasing annoyance. At this rate, she'll be here till noon.

Everyone stiffens when a new customer (Spanish?) enters and tries to sit down out of order. When someone near the door precedes an explanation with an elbow, he leaves with a few sour words (yes, Spanish). Everyone relaxes again, checking their watches and glaring one and all at that tiresome woman still signing her name. It grows noticeably warmer. Time creeps. Cecily understands time creeping. Number Two finally finishes, but Number Three takes just as long.

It is after that tiresome second customer that Cecily notices an itching about her ankles and behind her knees. Scratching is a great temptation, but she knows once she begins she won't be able to stop; it's never possible. Besides, her fingernails are already grimy from the ride into the bazaar and scratching with them would be incredibly risky. Instead, she uses the book to fan her legs and ankles.

Cecily begins to itch in less fannable places. Hoping that it is her overheated imagination, she frowns and ignores the discomfort. She tries to find something positive to think about but fails. She squirms quietly, trying to alleviate the itch in her panties by shifting her bottom on the chair. This helps as long as she's moving, but she can't squirm too long at a time without drawing unwanted attention.

Too soon, her pubic hairs feel like a herd of beasties are swarming, and her nipples begin to burn as if dipped in Tabasco. Brushing each arm across her chest, she pretends to push back wayward curls. Then, glancing out of the corners of her eyes at her companions in line and finding no one watching, Cecily Havenshack dares to rub her thighs together.

Anna warned her about this: fleas, lice, scabies, ticks! Her mouth droops, her eyes flutter as she resists scratching. There are only five people ahead of her now, but she doesn't know if she will make it. Still, if she abandons her position in line, the fleas will simply flee with her.

She would have to run to the American compound's over-chlorinated pool and jump in fully clothed and make a complete fool of herself, after which she would have to return to the bank for two thousand rupees.

One of her immediate neighbors must breed this vermin. To the left is a shapeless woman (French? No, Italian) wearing saffron pantaloons, a tie-dyed undershirt and layers of silver jewelry from every stop between Europe and Kathmandu. Cecily can't believe this female considers herself dressed! She herself has on an airy blouse of deep cinnamon with minute pleats tucked just so into the camel-colored split skirt, and she does not consider herself overdressed for a trip to the bank. Clearly this female is a likely source for whatever is burrowing due south of Cecily's waist.

Everyone shifts to another chair, leaving her only four people away from her servants' wages. She takes advantage of the shuffle for some surreptitious scratching, then eyes the man on her right — Number Eight.

Well, he appears normal enough. Sedately garbed in khaki slacks and a beige camp shirt, a clean knapsack at his feet, he is reading a book. That alone is reassuring. He holds the book with his left hand, his right arm hanging straight down out of sight on his other side. She tries to read the title at the top of the page, but it is in formal German with those incomprehensible capitals. She watches as he puts the book on his lap and slaps at his neck. He blandly meets Cecily's suspicious eye before refocusing on his book.

Her crotch prickles with a creeping fire. There are still four people to go. No, only three. They all move a seat closer to getting their money, Cecily again scratching vigorously in the shuffle. The relief is wonderful but too temporary. Three more, three more, and she is going in that swimming pool fully clothed no matter who is watching.

In truth, Cecily grows more indignant with herself as her discomfort increases. Deeply ingrained middle class manners forbid her to touch her privates except in absolute solitude, and she is torn at this moment: she should have enough gall to scratch her privates if need compels, especially considering the present company. There! That woman across the room, the one in see-through muslin and all those tattoos, the one casually scratching her breast! If that woman can scratch privates in public, then Cecily Havenshack can, too.

Five hundred new fleas suddenly arrive and she squirms violently on the chair, knocking the book out of her neighbor's hand.

"Sorry."

She bends to pick it up, groping overlong on the floor while allowing herself an awkward rubbing on the smooth wood chair. Flushed, she straightens and hands the book to Number Eight, who offers thanks in a distinctly American accent.

Far too soon whatever vermin that female, Number Ten, is breeding again torture Cecily. She can barely restrain herself from reaching under her skirt, and she groans softly, causing Number Eight to glance sideways. Cecily fans her flushed face, the breeze turning a page of his book.

"Sorry!"

"Don't mention it," he answers with a hint of a Southern drawl.

The traveler at the desk finds out that he will have to go to another branch to solve his particular financial dilemma, and he stomps out muttering in Dutch. Everyone shifts over one seat, allowing her another fleeting respite, but within moments she knows she won't be able to hold out any longer. She has to scratch, she has to scratch now. And not just a brief little scratch but a digging in and rooting out of an itch rapidly driving her mad.

Lowering her eyelids, she glances quickly around the room. She senses this is a diplomatically unimportant group, a group of invisible people. Good. So. Are any of these unimportant people looking her way? Yes! That new man last in line across the room. Yes? No. He is just stoned and vacantly staring in her direction. Ok then. That's all right. Everyone else appears intent on their own method of enduring this tedious wait. Feeling a measure of safety, she thinks maybe she can do it; no one seems aware of her existence, and none of them mean anything to her anyway, do they? Of course not. The man at her right continues reading. The woman on her left could be dead, it has been so long since she's even blinked.

Slowly Cecily lifts her hand from its death grip on the edge of the chair, her frantic eyes keeping a wide angle focus on the room. Then, holding her breath, she breaks a lifetime prohibition on touching her privates in public and lets her hand steal toward the center of her lap. Her hand hovers there for a moment while she sweeps the room one last time, then drops straight down. She begins to scratch, to dig harder and deeper, uprooting that itch.

God, the relief of it! She closes her eyes in bliss as she continues digging, her head lolling back against the wall.

Even with her eyes shut, Cecily notices the change in the light of the room. Someone is standing in the doorway. One last scratch before she looks, and it takes a moment of blinking before she can focus.

When she does, her eyes, glittering green, and his, black like no one she's ever known, meet. Black eyes that brood from both sides of his memorable nose. Cecily will certainly never forget that nose, those stormy eyes. That mouth once again laughing at her. Oh my god!

In the lightning movement of her hand up from between her

thighs, she once again knocks Number Eight's book out of his hand to the filthy floor. She gasps, still mesmerized by the man in the door, as Number Eight exclaims, "Well! Really!"

As she scrambles for the book, blood suffuses her face. She turns to her right and tumbles into an incoherent apology, keeping her face averted from that odious beast still filling the door.

Number Eight is nonplused but responds politely when she addresses him as if an old buddy. She really takes no notice that he never moves his right arm. She is too busy avoiding the man in the door who caught her kneading her privates in public to notice very much about this other man, or even to remember his name when he tells her twice.

With her itch miraculously cured, she moves to the next chair and is still in the black-eyed man's direct line of sight. She titters hysterically at Number Eight's mildest remark and, like a fool, pretends great interest in his pleasantly offered information.

After her traveler's checks are finally cashed and she stumbles from the room, she finds Number Eight waiting for her outside. It appears she agreed to lunch with him, though she has no recollection of doing so. However, since he chases away two beggars from her bicycle, she feels the least she can do is share a meal with a fellow American whose right arm doesn't move even once. Besides, panicking at the thought that the other, even stranger man will soon emerge from the bank to find her still here, she will agree to almost anything just to get away without attracting any more attention.

She's also disconcerted because she can't remember this nice man's name even though he's mentioned it a third time. Fortunately, she does remember she has to go straight home to pay her employees. Backing the bike away, she agrees to meet for dinner instead. The bank door opens as Cecily merges with New Road traffic less cautiously than normal.

12

AFTER A SLEEPY AFTERNOON in a blessedly quiet palace, Cecily trudges back up to the bazaar, heading for the Kathmandu Guest House. She explains to herself that keeping this date with Number Eight can be viewed as gratitude. It can be seen as touching base with a fellow American, and after all these years abroad she is certainly in need of catching up with her own culture. She forces herself to walk faster.

Coming to a fork in the path, she stands undecided. The short cut to town is always beyond squalor, and the last time she took it was too horrible an experience to repeat any time soon. The longer road to town is a far more peaceful option. While she walks a light drizzle fills the air and no taxis are in sight. Pushing up the steel spring of her Hong Kong golf umbrella, she continues briskly toward the left turn that leads down to the Bishnumati River before winding up to the bazaar.

Pigs and dogs feed on abundant night soil on both sidewalk and riverbank as she carefully picks her way down this offal-littered road, crowded with picturesque old buildings and tiny shops. Her favorite business on the riverside street sells posters of Hindu gods, where as usual she is drawn to the images of a slick blue Krishna, all voluptuous curves and his trademark mustache, and she decides to buy one next time she has any money.

She makes her way toward an old bridge that spans the Bishnumati. Beyond it, the road continues up into the bazaar. Cars squeeze by pedestrians, motor scooters blast by pushcarts, and it is a miracle the bridge continues to stand under such an onslaught. The whole thing will cave in someday, soon probably, for the river seems more swollen than usual this early into monsoon. With this thought in mind, Cecily approaches the bridge with trepidation. Today her timing is not good.

As she weaves into rush hour traffic crossing the sagging structure, vehicles nosing through keep her distracted, so she does not notice a short parade of men dressed in filthy rags crossing from the other side. She bumps into the ragged man leading this procession just about mid-bridge. Her umbrella knocks off his *topi.* Stepping back, she is struck a glancing blow by a rickshaw. She regains her balance and steps forward again. This brings the procession of ragged men to a halt, effectively paralyzing all traffic on the bridge which bulges alarmingly.

She realizes she is the epicenter of a traffic jam. Around her, smells and noise increase every time she breathes. A taxi beeps shrilly behind her; curls stick to her damp forehead. She knows she mustn't faint, not here, so she pants while holding on to that thought.

When she next looks up, it is straight into the soles of a very dead man, who is being carried all wrapped up in white cloth by this procession of ragged men. One meter from her face and closing, these are the soles of a brutal life lived barefoot. Now dead, they are food for new nightmares.

Cecily retches, losing the remains of her lunch. People around watch with interest this memsahib vomiting on the bridge. Wiping her mouth with a delicately embroidered hankie, she stammers an incoherent apology and reels around the funeral procession and on through suddenly moving traffic. She staggers up a steep hill toward the edge of the bazaar.

Later, calm again, Cecily focuses on her dinner date. What is his name? Why can't she remember his name? Deciding there is no choice but to ask at the hotel desk, she once again puts Number Eight out of her mind as she enters the bazaar for the second time this day.

At Kathmandu's heart stand the eerie wood pagodas of Dhurbar Square. She skirts the edge of the square, noting all the odd architectural shadows the pagodas create. These particular pagodas make her uneasy even in daylight, so dusk is a challenge to her common sense, as it always has been. She is reassured a bit when she passes a neighborhood band just getting warmed up in the west corner of Dhurbar Square. Harmonium music hangs in the air, follows her like a companion as she leaves the square, heading north past the toothache shrine and eventually out of the bazaar.

The Kathmandu Guest House sits at the end of a long driveway past trekking gear shops and rug merchants in a predominantly Tibetan neighborhood. She glances into these prosperous businesses, but sees nothing she has not seen before. She turns and walks up the drive with dragging feet.

When Cecily enters the lobby of the Kathmandu Guest House, her plan to ask at the desk for Number Eight's real name is thwarted. Number Eight from Room Thirty-three is standing in the lobby waiting for her.

"Cecily! Hello!"

Startled, she blurts, "Oh, shit!" then burbles in embarrassment, "Uh, I didn't want to see you there — I mean, I didn't expect you to be waiting here. For me."

He politely ignores her stupidity.

"I thought I'd better wait down here." He adds shyly, "I'm glad you came."

"Uh, thank you."

There is an awkward silence in which Cecily pretends great interest in the uninteresting lobby. She can see a garden through the back where guests are sitting. She struggles to think of something intelligent to say, finally asking, "So, where would you like to eat?"

He says uncertainly, "Well, I saw this sign, the one there on the wall? For a show and dinner, and I thought that might be fun. If you'd like to go?"

"Uhm."

"It starts at seven, if that's all right?"

"Uhm. Well. We should get going then."

He starts away and up the stairs, one arm motionless, then turns back to ask, "Would you like to come up, to see my room?"

She pivots the opposite direction, calling over her shoulder,

"No! I mean, I think I'll wait in the garden."

There is laughter in his voice when he says, "Right. I'll be back."

As he disappears around the corner of the stairwell, Cecily, who is watching from the corner of her eye while striding for the garden door, abruptly wheels back to the front desk, moving her chin for the clerk's attention.

"Excuse me, could you tell me that man's name? The guest in Room Thirty-three?"

After studying this memsahib for signs of criminal intent, the clerk flips through his register, finally saying, "Thirty-three? Thirty-three, ok, Mr. S. Morgenstern, USA."

"S?"

"Yes, Mr. S. Morgenstern, USA."

Cecily mutters her thanks and stares at the floor. S? S? Samuel? Scott? Morgenstern is Jewish, isn't it? Or is it German? Solomon? Serge? Saul, Seth, Sebastian? Sinbad, Scaramouche ...

She walks out into the garden, which stretches a surprising distance. Chairs are scattered about, some occupied, everyone quietly alone in the evening light. Finding two chairs empty and together, she plops down and looks around. Behind her sits a large statue of Buddha with an enormous cactus growing up around it. She shudders and settles more deeply into the cane-sprung chair.

S. Morgenstern reappears in the lobby, his left hand holding a camera while his right hangs loose to his side. Cecily grits her teeth when he disturbs a woman standing nearby, asking her to take their photo. He focuses the lens with single-handed dexterity, hands over the camera with a set of explicit instructions, then pulls the empty chair closer to Cecily's. Buddha looms behind them. Studying S.'s right arm while he is turned away, she can see no gory details through the sleeve of his safari jacket. Besides this, she still can't remember his name. The shutter clicks, the camera is handed over, and Cecily says, "Ready, Mr. Morgenstern?"

"What? Oh, that's good. Mr. Morgenstern, ha!"

"Ha ha," echoes Cecily glumly, then she hastily adds, "About this show, do you think we could just go somewhere for a quiet dinner? Perhaps some curry at The Other Room?"

He turns to her with an unsure smile on his face. "Well, I already bought the tickets. Earlier this afternoon."

"Oh, I see. Then that settles it."

She smiles reassuringly at his awareness of a poor choice. Inexplicably, her gloomy mood begins to lift. Really, he is charming, a sort of innocent abroad, she thinks. Again, her gaze briefly rests on his right sleeve. Averting her eyes, she asks, "Where is this show?"

"It's at the, wait a sec, at the Radjoot Hotel? A Himalayan dance troupe?"

"Dance? Oh, then that's all right, I thought maybe it was a movie or a play. The dance shows are usually tolerable. And afterwards we could go to a restaurant I know that's quite near there."

S. Morgenstern shifts uncomfortably, saying, "They have this dinner there. Nepali food? And I thought that we could, that is, I told them that we would probably eat there."

His eyes are brown and very kind. Cecily gives in good-naturedly.

"Nepali food? That's classic, let's go!"

His smile shows even white teeth and crinkles around his eyes. Suddenly she feels much better about a dinner of rice, lentils and goat. She automatically smoothes her frock, checking for cane snags, and pushes her curls off her face. S. Morgenstern gestures for her to precede him through the lobby. She notices that his right arm doesn't swing free as he moves, and she is relieved he has some control over it. Perhaps it is simply sprained, or bound down? She shifts her attention back to what he is saying.

"I want to thank you right now for spending this evening with me. I know you must be busy with your life here, so I appreciate you sharing some time with me."

She forces herself to relax as S. Morgenstern leaves his camera at the desk and follows her out into the monsoon evening. He really is a sweetheart, so what is his bloody name? Stephan? Steve? Simon? Stanley?

Irritated, she blows curls out of her eyes. Satchel? Safford? Shane — no, definitely not Shane.

Giving up, she takes a deep breath, turns and smiles brilliantly at S., causing him to stumble as he walks, his arm that moves reaching up to grab her arm, quickly letting go. It is after this stumble that she notices S. Morgenstern also has a limp.

They take a cab to the Radjoot. By now Cecily has resigned herself to the show, but she casts one more vote against Nepali food.

"Perhaps you'd like to try some of the best Russian food in the world?"

He frowns, clears his throat, declining the opportunity.

13

THEY CAN BARELY HEAR THE MUSIC because of rain drumming on the roof. After the final dance concludes, they slosh from the performance pavilion to the chilly lobby painted sky blue and filled with gray chairs. Facing the prospect of lentils and goat curry for dinner, Cecily squares her shoulders. She dislikes lentils only slightly less than goat, but S. Morgenstern is not going to hear one more peep from her.

They drip across the lobby to join other guests waiting outside the dining room's locked door. S. Morgenstern recognizes tourists up from India that he'd met at the post office just this very day. After effusive greetings, they discuss the merit of the dancers, the authenticity of the dancers, the costumes of the dancers, and yes, they certainly enjoyed it very much, indeed!

Cecily concentrates on not scratching mosquito bites behind her knees. She fans humid air with her damp and tattered dance program, as they all continue to stand at the dining room's locked door, which shows no sign of opening any time soon. The discourse on each dancer's merit continues unabated, except when Cecily interrupts to inquire pointedly about the delay with dinner. But everyone is having such a good time, yes, such a very good time, that they all agree it must be well worth the wait.

She decides right then and there that if S. Morgenstern asks these, these shoppers up from Delhi, no doubt, to join them for dinner, she will march straight out this door. Well, maybe that door over there.

At this very moment, S. Morgenstern glances uncertainly between Cecily and the beaming Hindi tourists and opens his mouth to speak. Quickly, Cecily steps between S. and the others, calling out much too loudly, "Manager!"

Much, much too loudly, indeed. Then, from between S. and the Delhi matron in her actually rather lovely chiffon *sari,* Cecily shouts at the men behind the reception desk, "Why is the dining room still locked?"

The manager pauses amid a whispered disagreement with the desk clerk. He turns to this memsahib so loud in his lobby. He replies with great dignity that the restaurant has been unavoidably closed for the evening. Cecily rolls her eyes toward the curious Hindi cherubs painted on that one too cerulean wall. She turns back to S. Morgenstern, saying much too brightly, "Closed! Oh, isn't that too bad!"

S. Morgenstern watches her with an odd expression on his kind face, and Cecily blushes. She studies her toes.

"So, what would you like to do, Cecily."

He sounds tired. She looks up with embarrassed, apologetic eyes.

"Why don't we go somewhere just to eat and talk. Anywhere. Anyhow, I'm almost starved, Mr. Morgenstern."

Laughter makes him handsome. He gestures with his good arm, "Of course, Mrs. Havenshack. If you will excuse us?" And he bows them away from the actually quite decent family up from Delhi.

Because it is raining harder, Cecily and S. huddle close under her umbrella. Always his left side is to her, as they wait and wait for a taxi to arrive. None arrive. After standing far too long in the cold rain, they risk a drenching and run for the hotel's long, dark driveway leading back to the main road. When they're halfway down this gloomy drive, the sky empties itself in a mind-numbing downpour.

Although they try to stay under her umbrella, Cecily's cotton frock grows heavy and clings to her legs. Unable to see, she steps into a puddle that goes up past her knees. Off balance, she totters away through the water, leaving her companion exposed in the deluge. At that moment her umbrella catches a gust and drags her through the muddy pool, then springs inside out. The wind helps S. slosh forward, and he reaches out to grab Cecily close. They struggle on blind, clutching each other.

Then, in a copse of pine trees that shelters them, they stand panting and holding on to each other. Cecily feels S. Morgenstern lean closer, and she lifts her chattering lips thinking he is about to sweep her into his arm, but instead he sways dangerously.

Floundering to keep her balance, she reaches around his waist to steady him as he leans heavily against her. She loses her grip on the umbrella, which falls into the dark water. As she bends to retrieve it, S. almost topples over. Quickly she braces all her weight against him. She staggers but holds. Craning sideways she looks down, but her umbrella has disappeared.

S.'s face glows blue-white and hollow-eyed in dim visibility. Knowing they will fall over if they stand there any longer, Cecily shouts at S., "Move!" She gives him a little shove, and S. steps forward uncertainly. He staggers a few more steps, but she keeps a good grip on his arm. Then, thinking he is stable again, she bends and gropes just once more in the thick, inky water for her umbrella, but S. staggers sideways and she has to splash after him, abandoning the favorite Hong Kong umbrella to its murky grave.

As suddenly as it began, the downpour stops. They now stand on a small island in a long black lake where the hotel driveway used to be. He breathes easier, stands straighter, his left hand up over his eyes. It appears that he might be praying. She whispers, "Are you all right?"

No answer. She whispers again, "Can I do something to help?"

This time the sound of her voice and the touch of her hand on his arm draw him back to their muddy mess. He shakes his head, flinging drops of water, then he focuses long into her finally honest eyes. He smiles.

As they move a few faltering steps, Cecily murmurs encouragement, supporting him as lightly as possible. He offers a curt apology that breaks her heart.

What she says out loud is, "Been needing a good rain, don't you think?"

"What rain?" he gasps, grabbing her hand and squeezing it as he takes stock of the ominous lake lapping at their tiny island. "How far to the street, do you think?"

"Just a short swim. Can you, I mean, do you want to try it?"

He looks at her. Clearly, whatever caused pain so severe he leaned on her of all people, whatever it was has subsided, and he replies firmly, "Of course I can make it. Come on!"

They troop off into the water. It is deeper for her because she's shorter. When they reach the main road, S. Morgenstern is again sheet-pale and shivering. They stagger down the street hoping for a taxi, deciding to return straight to the Kathmandu Guest House for towels from his room. Cecily shivers stoically in her dripping dress.

14

STEIN? SKIP? SPIKE? SAGE? NO. Cecily dredges up every S. name in the known world, yet not one clicks. Meanwhile, S. sits across a battered table in a Chinese-Tibetan restaurant filled to bursting with loud tourists and no Tibetan or Chinese.

Before this, they visit his room to towel off. When she catches sight of herself in the wavy mirror, she is humbled by the pathetic reflection. She descends to the lobby while S. changes into dry clothes. At first he insists on staying wet, if she doesn't change then he won't either, but Cecily pushes him back into his room telling him not to be ridiculous, although she does accept a jacket that he drapes over her shoulders. It dwarfs her, and now S. Morgenstern sits and watches her with an arrested look while they order mixed up Chinese food. She fidgets as they wait. She babbles. She asks him about the drawl in his voice.

"Are you from the South?"

He smiles, "Is it so obvious?"

"It's scarcely there, just certain words you say. Like the way you say 'woman.' And when you mean 'pull' you say 'pool.' Words like that."

"You know a bit about this particular accent, I take it?" He adds, leaning forward, "I myself have always been fascinated with language and speech."

Pleasure surges at this, and Cecily admits, "Well, I studied linguistics a bit in college."

Relieved that she's hit upon a topic of strong mutual interest, she launches into an exploration of certain theories on the migration of languages. Eventually grinding to a halt in the face of his bemused attention, she stares at the empty table. Oh my god, did she say all that? Peeping up at him, she finds another odd expression on his very nice face.

She suddenly realizes that S. makes her feel better about herself than she does with other people. Even better than she feels about herself around her own husband, what with his comments that could be compliments or insults: she never knows for sure.

And she knows for certain she feels safer with S. than anywhere near that other man. That man in the bazaar, the one with the unforgettable nose and those strange obsidian eyes that strip her dry to the bone every time they meet. She glares again at the Formica table.

"Is something wrong?"

"What? Oh! No, no, I just thought of something. Nothing."

The conversation turns to travel. Cecily finds herself enjoying S.'s gently caustic wit. As steamed *momos* arrive, S. reaches Australia.

"One place I like more than most, for the beer I admit, is Australia. Was there in their winter, around '68, on a medical R & R, a shrapnel problem."

He stops in surprise, then grins somewhat ruefully. It is an "I didn't mean to say that" look. She controls her curiosity by diligently chewing chow mein.

He continues, "Beautiful country, whole continent to itself. Shouldn't imagine ever feeling crowded there. After I was up to speed again I spent most of my time in the Northern Territory looking for crocodiles, camera stuff, and sitting in the sun getting tight with some real fine people, real straight-in-the-eye folks."

Cecily shivers under a puffing air conditioner in the wall above them. She lifts her cold dress off her legs. Beginning to ache from her neck down to her lower back, she feels she must keep the conversation going, if only because S. is looking so much better now. His color is good again and his eyes sparkle. Her voice trembles only slightly as she asks, "What about the cities like Melbourne and Sydney, and —"

Her mouth agape, she stares at him. Of course! Of all the bloody fools! That's his name! His name is Sidney! Isn't it?

It sounds right, but, but, oh dear! Perhaps not. Sidney? Sidney. Since getting to know him better, she has almost decided upon Simon, or maybe Stephen, something with quiet dignity. She stares at him: Simon, Stephen, yes. But Sidney?

Seeing the open amusement in his eyes, Cecily stumbles on, "And! And, uh, Melbourne?"

"Melbourne's fine, a fine city. Enjoyed myself there."

She mumbles a question about Sydney.

"Sydney? My namesake? Well, to look at, it was all right. Clean, you know. But can't say I had the best time of my life there. And I haven't seen Perth. Missed a lot, Australia's big, you know."

The waiter brings one of the dishes and they divide it, wolfing their food while the air conditioning wheezes over them. Cecily shivers more and more frequently as the meal progresses. Trying to suppress these small convulsions has given her a bit of a headache. A particularly severe series of shakes makes her go pale. She draws his jacket closer around her shoulders.

"I do prefer Sid, Cecily."

She reddens up to the roots of her damp hair. Damn! He knew. He'd known all along that she'd forgotten his name again. Why didn't she ask when it was still appropriate back at the beginning of the evening? She mumbles, "I'm sorry."

"You should be."

But he smiles as he says it. She puts both her hands back on the table. When he reaches for them with his one good arm, he grows immediately concerned over their iciness.

"Here, here! This won't do!"

"Oh, it's all right, I'm fine, really."

She punctuates this with a sneeze, so he pays no attention to her protests, calls for the bill, and sweeps her out into a night still cool but not as wet. She makes feeble disclaimers to being chilled as they head toward the lobby and the stairs and his room. He ignores her, saying, "I have just the thing to warm you up."

She is racked by a shiver ending in another sneeze. Sid manages the stairs quickly even with his one leg dragging. Unlocking the door to Room Thirty-three takes but a moment; he does it all with one hand. They enter his small room with its small bed, small bureau, and closet for short clothes. The tiny sink stands alone in one corner.

"Here, take off that dress."

"Mr. Morgenstern!"

"Come on, come on! Take it off."

He is rummaging in his suitcase with his back to her. What is he looking for? Something to warm her up from his suitcase? Her voice quavers, "Sidney?"

"Now where is it?"

Standing always with his good arm to her, he searches the cabinet above the sink, then he moves to the bureau and opens one drawer after another. Her nethers tingle, which makes her cross her hands over her wet but dressed chest and protest, "Sid? Really, I don't think—"

"Here! Now, why did I stick it there?"

He stands with his back to her, something in his good hand that has a long cord trailing on the floor. Her mouth goes dry.

"Memory's getting rotten."

He turns, exclaiming, "Cecily." He laughs, "Mrs. Havenshack, I can't very well dry your dress with you inside it."

Cecily peers closely at the appliance in his hand: a blow dryer. Slowly she looks back up to find Sid with a sad smile on his wonderful, homely face.

"You have nothing to worry about, hon."

"Oh."

Cecily tries to cover the disappointment in her voice by laughing, "If you could imagine what I was thinking!"

They smile across the small space, then stop too soon. Sid bends and lays the blow dryer on the floor and reaches with his good arm to plug the appliance in under the bureau. In order to do so, he has to unplug the one lamp, leaving the room dappled by temple lights outside the small windows.

Silence is broken by the rustle of her dress falling to the floor. Sid reaches for the dress as he stands and clucks with concern that she was wearing it so wet and cold. He wrings it out with one hand, then he tells her to hold it up while he turns the blow dryer on.

Her reluctance to remove her dress lies somewhat in the fact that she wears no bra. But, deciding she is not ashamed of her breasts, she has only two and they are smallish and roundish and synchronized against her chest, she decides she'd rather have a dry dress than pneumonia.

Anyway, Sidney is clearly intent on spraying her dress with hot air. Cecily holds up the frock and turns it, watching him, her eyes unknowingly big, her nose warm and snuffly. Sid looks over at her flushed cheeks, lingers on her breasts and travels down to her white cotton panties made transparent from rain. She does not offer them to his blow dryer.

The dress revolves, the machine blows. Her frock is drying all too quickly. Soon it will be out of her hands. It will be back on, and then what will she do.

As usual, she shrinks from making any overture, but Sid could make one anytime now and she would duly consider it for many reasons. She would consider it first because here she is. No one even knows she's standing in a man's bedroom in a hotel, almost nude already so what's the big deal. Even if he can't do it, they could do other its.

Second, he would probably never come to Kathmandu again, and if he did come she would possibly not see him, their first meeting had been such a chance occurrence. But if he did come back to Kathmandu and they did meet, she would most likely not be with Stewart, she was hardly ever with Stewart. If by chance they did meet while she was with Stewart, well, Sidney Morgenstern is obviously a gentleman, and this is clearly her opportunity to have that affair with no one the wiser. Well, maybe not an actual affair, what with the shrapnel and all.

But anyway. Here it is. The big opportunity. Better even than the one Stewart and Joel arranged, she thinks smugly as she watches Sidney Morgenstern blow her dress.

She feels, standing there in her undies, what one could call stirring desire move along her flanks. Cecily is urged by this sensation to deflower herself once and for all. What would S. Morgenstern feel like against her body? What would he whisper in her ear when he settled between her legs? Would he actually be able to do anything? Then, there is his strange right arm, and his leg that drags a little. Are they fake? Would he take them off and put them on the floor by the bed?

Continuing to hold up the dress and turn it in hot wind, she stands lost in thought. Suddenly, off goes the electricity, back on, flickering, then dimming to a brownout. The blow dryer splutters to a halt, and in the silence she hears Sid click it off. She drops her arms, just now aware of what a considerable strain it has been to hold up the dress all this time.

Sidney Morgenstern asks, "Does the power usually come back on?"

"It could. Sometimes it does."

"Well. Your dress must be close to dry anyway."

"Yes, yes it is."

"Hmm. Would you like a flashlight?"

Declining his offer of yet another appliance, Cecily sighs, "No. That's all right."

She begins dressing in the dark. Her dress is warm.

15

FOR THE NEXT SIX DAYS it rains solidly, steadily, constantly, unvaryingly and uniformly, a firm deluge of grand proportion. Rice fields are emerald under low, smokey skies.

On the seventh morning, the sun emerges. One of the maids floats flowers in copper bowls and sets them in each room. Shutters are folded back in all the rooms, wrought iron balconies dappling daylight onto the polished wood of the old floors.

Suddenly, the sparsely furnished, enormous rooms are teased by a stirring in the air. Startled by the sensation across her skin, Cecily walks outside. Wings of the palace embrace a private flower garden, a magical place that she rarely visits. Staring at the sky, she decides it really is going to clear. She smiles and stretches, touches her toes, holds the pose, breathes deeply and opens her eyes. She is face to face with a black ropey garden snake, and she screams all the way back inside.

The dreaded cry "*Naga!*" rises around the estate and everyone comes running with weapons in hand. As the unfortunate snake is bludgeoned to nonexistence, Preema helps Cecily calm down by brushing her hair one thousand full strokes. Recovered from hyperventilating, she decides to go lie in the rare monsoon sun at Phora Dhurbar, the American recreation compound. She grabs a basket and stuffs it with towels and a crossword puzzle, deciding not to take a book to read. Lately she's been reading two and three books a day; even her dreams have plots, so enough of other people's stories for a while.

Cecily pulls on her new maillot. She tugs at the sides where it splices up her honey-brown hips in that high French cut. Tilting curls out of her eyes, she inspects her reflection and frowns. She turns from the mirror and digs in the closet for a khaki memsahib-skirt, slips it over the maillot, then walks down a row of blouses, finally choosing a peasant shirt she'd had made in Denpasar in 1971. There, perfect.

Later in the taxi she regrets not bringing a book. Because of having no distraction, she anxiously assists the driver in navigating their vehicle. She exclaims in terror, "*Bistaare jaanos!*"

The driver slows ever so slightly. Cecily shrieks, "*Bistaare, bistaare jaanos*, you asshole!"

Turning to stare at her, the driver almost flattens a toddler. Hell! Cecily squeezes shut her eyes and pants. She hadn't meant to get upset, she knows it's no use, getting upset accomplishes nothing here. Opening her eyes to speak rationally to the cab driver she panics and screeches, "Here, here! Stop, goddamn you to hell!"

Trembling, she pays the fare and stumbles out of the taxi, which takes off before she closes the door. Then she trips on the curb at the gatehouse and limps into Phora Dhurbar past the impassive stares of the guards. The pool's rectangle of turquoise water is a welcome sight. Dropping onto the first chaise lounge in view, she settles back and closes her eyes. Time passes with the lazy lob of tennis on the nearby court and water lapping at the edge of the pool.

"Cecily?"

Cecily tugs up her suit as she squints past reflections from the pool shimmering under noon's hot, dense glare.

"Cecily! Over here!"

Turning, she spots Anna, whom she hasn't seen for weeks. As usual, Anna draws everyone's eyes as she moves with long-legged ease through the loungers toward Cecily. As usual, her friend appears not to notice everyone is staring.

Carelessly dropping her things to the hot cement, Anna drapes herself across a lounge, legs stretching a mile before ending at high-gloss red toenails. As Anna raises her exotic face to the sun, Cecily lowers her sunglasses and peers past them: her own legs, though shapely, are clearly those of a different species. She sighs and shoves the sunglasses back up her nose.

For her whole life, everyone's considered Cecily so cute, such a bitsy-button of a girl who surely couldn't be old enough to drive! To vote! To get married! Her lack of height has made others consider her a wisp of a woman, a female of no firm substance.

Cecily thinks this crossly, as she eyes Anna's long legs and strong, unforgettable face. No one would ever call Anna wispy, even if her hair were fuzzy and fell in her eyes, which it doesn't. Her rangy beauty is the continual envy of every woman in town. They murmur among themselves when she enters a room, then exclaim, "That bag! Those shoes! Anna, where on earth did you get them?" Anna always laughs and lights a cigarette and blows smoke over their heads.

What's so odd is Anna's UN economist husband Jimmy, who stands a good ten centimeters shorter than his wife and sports a paunch besides. Cecily has always done Anna the favor of never questioning this. She and Anna have been best friends since first meeting at a faculty party years ago, and she would never trade having a best friend for the longest legs in the world.

"Is that coffee you're having?"

"No, tea, want some?"

Cecily looks vaguely around for the attendant. Anna waves a languid hand. "Don't bother, no rush. Got to camouflage my dark circles first."

She pulls out sunglasses and settles them on her elegant nose, their reflecting lenses adding luster to dark hair still damp from a recent shower. She yawns, moaning, "God, I'm tired."

Cecily tries to visualize dark circles behind Anna's lenses. She fails.

"Were you and Jimmy out late last night?"

Anna does not answer till she lights a match. She speaks around the cigarette between her lips, draws in the smoke, carelessly waves away the flame and drops the match by her chair.

"Jimmy's in Jumla, didn't you know?"

The way she says it, so casual with another wave of her hand, makes Cecily sit up straight. She glances around to see if anyone is close enough to hear them, while Anna watches the water move and smiles. Cecily leans forward.

"No, I didn't know. When did he leave?"

"Three days ago. Three blessed days ago."

Cecily's chair almost tips over as she leans even closer to her friend.

"Anna, tell me! What have you done?"

"Calmly, calmly, dear one. Hello, Macom, Sally. Nice day."

Cecily hadn't even heard the Schwartzes. She could swear Anna has a third eye open in an extremely convenient place. She fears Sally and Macom will pull over chairs to join them and there will go the opportunity to hear Anna's news, but Anna has the couple happily moving on, unaware they had been expertly manipulated into seeking a table on the other side of the pool. Cecily gapes in admiration.

Anna lies back with that enigmatic smile still in place and watches her cigarette smoke drift away. Peering closely, Cecily still can't see any dark smudges behind the sunglasses. She asks impatiently, "Well?"

"Yes?"

"Come on, Anna!"

Anna chuckles maddeningly. Then, she says she met him at the German ambassador's reception last Friday. A truly gorgeous man. Interest was piqued to a significant degree that very night, and she casually mentioned that Jimmy would be leaving for Jumla.

"Truly gorgeous?"

"Truly. Gorgeous."

Anna continues her story: when he called last night, she sent the servants away and had him for dinner. She stops talking, caught by a memory she isn't going to share, while her friend sits stunned, immobile. Then Anna continues, a funny twist to her lush mouth, "You know, if he'd had anything interesting to say, he would have been perfect. The avatar of all my fantasies," she sighs, then chuckles, "but conversation isn't his strong suit."

She glances at Cecily's expression and laughs, admitting, "Honey, I talk like I know what's what, but I've honestly never had an affair since Jimmy asked me to marry him. True blue, that's me. But this man? There's something about this man, I can't even explain it."

Anna tilts her head, staring right through Cecily. "He's incredible, like Tarzan. But, I don't know, something's not quite right. Something's missing."

Silence lingers while they mull this over. Cecily finally asks, "Will you see him again?"

"Oh, sure. Tonight."

Anna reaches down, crushing her cigarette into the cement, avoiding her companion's gaze.

"Then he leaves, never to return. Like I said, perfect."

Cecily considers this information, unaware of Anna's suddenly ragged look. She cautiously inquires, "Was he, uh, well, you know."

Anna laughs. "Yes, he was very you-know!"

"Oh."

To hide her confusion, Cecily stands and straightens her towel, then reclines. She thinks back to her own near affair. Near affair, ha! Near nothing but a head cold she'd just now recovered from, and blisters from a long walk home in wet shoes because the taxis were all running meterless, and on principle she refused to pay thirty rupees for an eight rupee ride even that late on that particular monsoon night. Near nothing is an apt description, and she never saw Sidney Morgenstern again.

Her reverie is broken by an enormous splash, then pandemonium. It turns out two of their teenage students have jumped into the pool from the roof of the snack kiosk. Cecily and Anna look at each other in disgust. The two vacationing teachers pick up their soaked belongings and retreat to a picnic table under a tree, toweling off and watching the irate crowd and abashed teens from a safe distance. They voice futile hopes that certain families will be reassigned before September and the beginning of another school year.

Clouds steal back through the radiant blue sky. Cecily feels a swift coolness spreading over her skin, so she stands and wraps her towel around under her arms. Glancing at her friend, she asks, "Well?"

Anna ignores her. Sighing, Cecily raises her hand to catch a passing waiter's attention but fails, so she scratches her scalp instead. Anna finally asks, "You want to know details?"

"Certainly I want to know details!"

Cecily means to take mental notes. She can study them before another opportunity arises. Anna laughs, lazily lifting her chin at a distant attendant who abandons someone else to hurry over. Cecily glares at the man, the same one who ignored her earlier.

"Tea? Coffee?"

Irritated, she petulantly snaps, "Nothing!" Seething till the waiter leaves, Cecily then leans toward Anna, "So? Come on, tell me. If *you* don't, how will I ever find out?"

Anna laughs again, while Cecily grits her teeth.

At this moment, Anna's partner on the day's tennis ladder shows up. Cecily veils her frustration as she smiles them off to the courts. She feels an urge for action, for movement toward her own adventure. But please, this time no gentlemen of such crippling kindness. And no blow dryers.

16

SHE STOPS ON THE CORNER to roll up her trouser legs. Last night came another heavy rain, leaving the road between her home and the charity clinic all puddles and mud. The sea of effluvia is almost enough to turn her back, except she is on her way to meet Anna at the clinic because Anna has that book for her. Anna had laughed, saying she would have it with her in a brown paper bag at the dispensary on Wednesday morning.

After sloshing out her drive and skirting blocks and blocks of mud, urine and feces, Cecily nears the clinic. From a distance she can see women sitting in a line straggling down the roadside. Their children lie beside them or stand with dirty bare bottoms and the swollen bellies of the truly malnourished. She watches the ground. She decides not to cross the street until just across from the clinic door.

The line is longer than usual, perhaps because monsoon is warm enough for people to wait so long to diagnose their hepatitis and last winter's pneumonia. There they sit guarding their children and keeping their places in line, some of them so ill they will very likely be dead by the fall festivals.

Cecily scolds herself for sleeping in just because of last night's slight headache. Her pain threshold is far too low because she was born lucky; neither misery nor squalor have callused her sensibilities.

She does think it odd about the clinic: here sit all these Nepalis seeking Western pharmaceuticals, while so many Westerners come here seeking Eastern cures. Yet, these same Westerners send their employees to the charity clinic for antibiotics and vaccines. People, Cecily decides, wincing her way over an especially foul patch of ground, are contradictory by nature.

She eases her way through the crowd at the door and into the hall and up two flights of stairs littered with people sniffling. Sneeze-cough-hack-hawk-spit bloody phlegm on the floor. It is evident from their clothes and jewelry that many of these women come from remote mountain tribes and have traveled for days, kilometer after kilometer with their children and not much else, not bus fare and not even shoes, to sit here in this line stretching out the door and down the street in monsoon's condensed heat. The ones inside are at least in the shade, though the air is already more foul than seems possible.

Pushing up the stairs, she meets resistance until the women turn and see she is a memsahib. Then a path miraculously opens before her. She eyes the floor, as much to avoid stepping in spit and whatever else is there as to avoid seeing the faces of all these people, and steps over a young girl lying across one riser.

The girl's eyes burn out of her pallor so intensely that Cecily can feel their heat. Stepping over someone is one of the biggest *jutos* in Nepal, like spitting in a well or kissing in public, but she is already committed and would have landed on the girl otherwise. Dismayed, she continues through the crowd and up the steps.

It grows more crowded and louder as she reaches the second landing where the line diverges into two rooms. She peeks through the closer door and sees one, then two, then a third Western spouse giving up her Wednesday to volunteer at the charity clinic. Problem is, the whole country qualifies for charity. These three women do not appear particularly benevolent, surrounded as they are by children held up by desperate, shoving mothers. The putrid taint of unwashed illnesses seeps deeper into her pores. Suddenly nauseated, she quickly backs away. Swallowing a rush of saliva, she weaves through more unhealthy people — is that a leper? My god! She shrinks toward the door in the opposite wall.

Again, as soon as the patients see who is pushing through they step aside without protest. Peering above this crowd, she can see Anna behind a window like a bank teller's. Anna is shouting at a tiny woman who cups a hand to her ear. Anna looks cool and distant in her white lab coat. Upon closer scrutiny, Cecily can see dark shadows around Anna's eyes: Another successful evening? When she calls, her friend looks up and waves her around to a side door.

"Hello, how are you!"

Anna turns away from a prematurely old girl holding up a slip of paper requesting pharmaceuticals to cure her of incurable ills.

"I am magnificently fine! How's that?"

Cecily laughs, buoyant, absorbing from Anna her smug contentment.

"Great! So where's the book? I must get right on this."

Anna shouts, "Yes, yes! Here, you are."

She reaches under the counter, brings out a paper bag and gives it to Cecily, then turns away with a shrug of "Sorry, busy, look at this mess." Calling out an unnoticed goodbye, clutching the book to her chest, Cecily fights her way back through the crowd to the landing, then down the stairs. It seems even more squalid after just those few minutes. When she comes upon that same skeletal girl lying on that same dank step, and now clearly unconscious, she hesitates. She looks around to see if anyone seems concerned for this pathetic person.

Impassive faces stare back and watch memsahib to see what she will do. No one wants to acknowledge an unknown girl dying on the stairs of the charity clinic. If they do, then they will become responsible for her body. They will have to cart it to the river and do *puja* and burn it.

She realizes that if she doesn't go back up and tell the volunteers about this girl, no one else will either, and then the volunteers will have to deal with a corpse. Resolutely, she turns and pushes her way back to the exit door by Anna's window.

"Anna. Anna!"

Anna turns, surprised to see her friend again.

"Look, there's this girl lying on the steps downstairs? I think she's unconscious. I don't know how bad off she is, but I don't think anyone is taking care of her. People just step right over her."

Anna's mouth tightens. Cecily adds uncertainly, "I just thought you should know."

"Holy fucking hell!"

"Can I do something to help?"

"God no, don't touch her! No telling what she has. I'll have one of the lab workers go down and see, he can get someone to help carry her up."

Cecily apologizes breathlessly in the face of Anna's reaction. "Sorry to bring bad news."

"This whole place is bad news!"

Seeing Cecily's astonishment, Anna's twisted mouth relaxes, breaking into a wry smile. "Just a little tired."

"Hey, sure! Are you positive I can't do something?" she asks as she edges away, paper bag clutched to her chest.

"No problem, stuff like this happens here. I just hope she isn't dead, it sets my co-workers into a panic. They think they're curing the entire mountain chain with their one day a week. Go on. Go on, get out of here! Enjoy your reading assignment."

Cecily shoves off again. Anna turns back to a pregnant teenager uncomplainingly waiting in a cold sweat on this hot day for the two memsahibs to finish talking.

17

THE BOOK IS NOT ONE Cecily would check out of any of Kathmandu's libraries. It is not a card she wants her name on, because people who check it out later would know she checked it out. This is mostly because of the illustrations.

After diligently reading the first two chapters, she realizes there is no need to be so methodical, so she begins to skip around in the book. In fact, skipping is one technique suggested. She slows down, placing the book on her lap.

Since Stewart thinks she needs practice, and Cecily herself is coming to see his point, then she will do it right. First, study illustrations of all those things she's never ever thought of till right now. Is this what Stew had hoped Joel would teach her?

Ok, that didn't work out. So she will learn on her own. That was how she learned Spanish in college, and she did quite well on the exams for never actually having been to Mexico or Spain.

Some of the suggestions in the book are astonishing. The old drawings in the first half are artistic; the photos in the second half suggest contemporary alternatives in, say, the position of a foot (lie it on its arch once it is over his right side) or details on how to spread the fingers of one hand to give symmetry to the entire position.

Really? Symmetry to a position? This section demands rereading. Well, perhaps that is of seminal importance and no one ever bothered to tell her? Stewart certainly never bothered. Symmetry, eh? Why not. She turns that page, then another.

By sunset she feels much as she did after finishing *Beowolf* back in college: she accomplished nothing applicable to her real life and possibly actually hurt her literate soul. *Beowolf* was debilitating because of the outmoded language and the archaic principles, among a ton of other problems in the cursed text. This Japanese sex book is crippling because it has filled her with lust when Stewart is in DC, Joel is in Calcutta, unless that is a lie too, and S. Morgenstern is dashing from Mandalay to Rangoon.

As usual alone, Cecily tries holding her fingers apart as she sips rum and cola in the sunroom on one more fading monsoon afternoon.

18

AFTER ANOTHER WEEK of sexy books and solitude, she understands the rains. She comes to know slow drizzles from slate skies as well as pounding cloudbursts just overhead, and she relaxes into monsoon and reads ten books in a row.

The palace stands empty. Its grounds spread out in perfect order with one lone gardener pulling weeds far down a row of cauliflower. Even Preema has been sent home, expected back next Monday. Before departing, Preema goes to the kitchen to check the amount of boiled and filtered water prepared for memsahib. This errand sends Cook into a snit. How dare she! they each claim, and Cecily is glad to see the backs of them all. Some of the staff she hasn't seen for weeks anyway.

On the eighth day when the sun reappears as a wet yellow light, Cecily peers out a window and scrutinizes the sky. Clouds hang moored to the foothills, but so far none are breaking loose across the valley. She puts aside her eleventh book.

In an effort to get herself back out into the peopled world, she makes plans to look for an orange bedspread for one of the guest rooms. Yes, orange, she decides. Those dark, heavy beams in that part of the palace need color. Promising herself a look-in at some of the shops along up Asan Tole, she exits the palace gates.

Late afternoon hums with energy released by sunlight. Weaving into the bazaar and around standing water, Cecily is quickly bored looking at bedspreads, even orange ones. Enough of this shopping already. Well, maybe just a quick glance in that one brass shop? But does she really need another old bronze candlestick? She slows, undecided. Pedaled vehicles push their way around her. Taxis honk like seals at the small of her back. She grits her teeth.

Irritated, she decides that shopping in Kathmandu has ceased to be an enjoyable pastime. After years of haggling with bazaar merchants, she daydreams about climate-controlled malls where clothes are off the rack. She hungers to push a cart down a dozen sparkling aisles where every item is packaged and clean. Best of all, absolutely no one would demand five times more just because she is a memsahib.

Mulling this over, trying not to let nostalgia grab hold and ruin her first afternoon outside for days and days, she walks up toward the end of Asan Tole. The crowds thin here. Traffic becomes a subtext to the ongoing hum of the bazaar.

It is then that she comes to the entrance of the Machendranath shrine. Obeying a strange impulse, she ducks into its low tunnel guarded by stone beasts. On the right as she passes through is a platform cut into the wall on which musicians perform and beggars sleep. There are three sleeping there now.

Cecily steps into sunlight slanting into the courtyard. Light throws complex shadows on a central temple and limns brick buildings on the far side of the square. Courtyard children tumble about, their games raucous. Pulled from play, urchins beg half-heartedly as she picks her way into a forest of icons surrounding the central pagoda.

Circling this holy structure, she keeps her right side respectfully to it. She understands the pagoda is actually Hindu, though there are a ton of Buddhas mixed in with all the Hindu icons. Hmm, hard to say. Intricately carved struts support an elaborate and layered roofline, which makes it very much a structure of the valley. She squints upward to see if the carvings are pornographic to ward off lightning — considered a virgin, lightning is appalled by pornography.

Back around toward the front, she pauses at a *yoni* on a pedestal with Buddhas carved around it. Now this she really doesn't understand. Buddha's vagina? She can't help but be amazed.

And then, as Cecily has remembered, near the entrance of the cobbled courtyard stands the oddest statue of the bunch, surely the oddest statue in Nepal, which Stewart pointed out on their very first tour of downtown Kathmandu.

Amid this polyglottic frieze of Asian beliefs, someone placed on a pedestal a Greek statue. The white marble nude holds her forehead with one hand, the other cupped modestly over her *yoni.*

Local Hellenophiles claim it is Io, a virgin raped by Zeus and then punished horribly by his jealous wife, Hera. The statue is clearly old and valuable, worthy of being stolen by Lord Elgin, but here it stands in the religious stew of the Machendranath temple. No one alive remembers how it ended up here.

The bowl at the stone woman's feet holds oil and a wick kept aflame day and night. Over the years, Cecily has observed Nepali women caring for this statue — sometimes Io wears flowers — so it doesn't seem to matter that the marble statue is Greek. As spiritual as the Nepalis are, Cecily feels it is all Greek to them, all these belief details brought in with each wave of conquerors and passage of dynasties.

As she passes Io's statue, Cecily touches it and touches her own forehead. She hurries to the exit, somehow spooked by her gesture.

Straightening as she steps out of the low passageway, she is met by the chaos of Asan Tole. Machendra's courtyard transported her back to a quieter, more mysterious Nepal; here and now again in Asan Tole, it takes a moment for her to reorient. Hmm. Well, shopping is definitely out, she decides, but to go home so soon would be to sink back into the iron lung of solitude. On this thought, she veers toward the King's palace. Maybe she'll try that new restaurant just past Air France?

She turns off the main road into an alley leading away from the deepest heart of the bazaar. As she walks down to where it meets Rani Pokhari with its clock tower beyond, she spots a favorite bookshop. Impulsively, she turns and bends inside through the entry, thinking she'll pick up a couple of used books, maybe a magazine.

She goes up steep steps at the rear of the ground floor, nodding to the owner, who is sipping tea and reading *The Rising Nepal*. She comes out into a second floor filled with foreign language publications. Two walls are lined with English books, one with French, and so on. She sees a shelf of new paperbacks from the PRC, which slows her momentarily, but then straight ahead are the maps and atlases, and she goes for that shelf without glancing farther around the room.

If she had looked to her left, she would have recognized the person standing by a window, reading about Sikh reverence for righteous violence.

Had she looked that way even briefly, Cecily would have turned and fled down the stairs and out the door, home to her solitude, and a lot more than a week would pass before she'd dare leave the palace again. But she didn't look.

PART III

ENTER NEMESIS

July, 1978

Prometheus

"She set Zeus's heart on fire with love and now she is violently exercised running on courses overlong ..."

19

THE UPPER FLOOR OF THE BOOKSTORE is crowded and musty, books spilling off shelves onto tables and rising in stacks across the old plank floor. Light filters through a carved Newar window looking out over traffic here at the bazaar's edge. Thumbing through a book of Tibetan maps, she purses her lips and blows a soft whistle of contentment through her nose. The old atlas is a gold mine of obscure connections between dialect and geography. Wonderful stuff!

The back cover shows no price marked, but a second book, an account of the wild journeys into Tibet of early missionary Annie Taylor, costs only thirty-six rupees. Deciding to take it for sure, she stuffs all the others back onto the shelf and turns toward the stairs. She will inquire how much this atlas costs, and perhaps she will buy both.

Turning, with a book in each hand, she has to stop because a man is standing right there just centimeters away. Surprised, even alarmed, Cecily looks up. She gasps when she recognizes his coal black eyes.

He grabs her, heaves her off her feet with her arms pinioned to her sides and her shoulders forced up to her chin, effectively locking her face into place in front of his. Two books hit the floor.

Later, Cecily imagines that if she had thought faster, she could have kicked him and maybe got away. However, it does not occur to her in this moment. She can only wonder if he is trying to replace her ears with her shoulders. His eyes remain obsidian smooth. She thinks briefly of the beauty of his nose, then of nothing else as he kisses her.

He kisses her very thoroughly indeed. Cecily does not close her eyes once during this kiss, but neither does he. This man works her mouth until he observes passion cloud over her panic, and then he releases her.

Her hand rises immediately to her lower lip. She brings it away with blood. He moves his gaze over her throat and face. She flinches when he reaches out and touches some wispy curls around her temples.

"So soft."

It is the first time she has heard his voice. The deep timbre she imagined would be there really is there. Amazing. He touches her arms where his fingers have left angry marks.

"Sorry," he says.

She continues staring dazedly up into those black eyes, his exceptionally fine nose separating them. Then she whispers, "I'm sorry, too," and brings her two fists together straight up into his scrotum, where Stewart taught her even she will do enough damage to gain a chance to escape.

Target found, she drives out all his air. He has not expected this. He doubles over and retches at her knees, but she does not retreat. Instead, Cecily grabs his ears and twists them both as hard as she can, which causes him to bend even more so she can push on his shoulders and force him flat to the floor. He is unable to defend himself for these few moments. He is almost unable to breathe. Stepping over him, she murmurs, "Don't move, I'll be right back," and then threads her way through the haphazard stacks to the creaky stairs.

At their bottom she finds the owner still sitting on a high stool reading the daily newspaper. She knows him, for she has come here many times before. She requests two cups of tea to be brought quickly from the nearest tea shop. A little confounded by her bloody appearance, but unwilling to deny a frequent customer two cups of tea, the shopkeeper noisily sends off one of his boys. Starting back up the stairs, she then turns and calls, "No sugar!" after the boy.

Preoccupied with the steep, dimly lit ascent, she remounts the stairway, dabbing at her lip. As she steps onto the second floor, a hand reaches out and grabs her ankle and pulls her leg out from under her. She falls sideways against a bank of shelves, then forward to the floor. From there, she is steadily pulled over the fallen books toward the man with black eyes.

Uh oh! He has recovered too quickly! Stewart claimed she should be able to put a man out of commission for at least five minutes, and she used all her power in that punch. Twisting around, Cecily stretches back toward the stairs, clawing at the shelves and worn matting, but her body hurts already and her strength is waning. He jerks her easily toward him.

She panics. Is he going to hit her? She fears that pain, that kind of pain, and it gives her a bit more impetus to claw back up the matting. He follows her a meter or so to get a better grip up her legs, and then, giving one strong tug, drags Cecily backwards so fast that her chin is floor burned and her lower lip is again squashed against her teeth. Tears blur her vision while he wraps his hand in the back of her blouse and pulls her till she is his. She feels herself roughly turned half-over. He has his hand clutching the front of her blouse like a bully in a movie. She goes limp and lets her head hang back to the matting. She looks straight up into eyes that have gone opaque.

They regard each other silently. Completely. A long stillness in that old room up there at the edge of the bazaar. She swallows, then offers through bloody lips, "I've ordered tea?"

Still holding her up with his fist turned in her clothes, he reaches with his other hand into his pocket, pulls out a bandana and wipes the blood off her face. Attempting not to wince, she winces anyway.

He growls, "You ok?"

"Yes. Yes, I think so."

The damage they've inflicted creates a livid closeness. She realizes he still has his fist doubled up in the front of her blouse like he is planning to swing her out the window.

"*Chiyaa*, memsahib," calls the boy clomping up the steps with two glasses of hot milky tea. The man holding her on the floor sits up and pulls her with him out of the pile of books just as the boy reaches them.

"*Chiyaa*, memsahib?" He holds out one glass.

"*Chini hoina?*"

"*Chini chha*, memsahib."

Cecily turns to the man lounging beside her with one arm tight on her shoulders. "They both have sugar."

"S'all right."

She nods at the boy. "Set them there."

The boy sets the glasses on the floor by all the spilled books, then he leaves. He says nothing: everyone knows *sahibs* and memsahibs have their own odd ways, not to be questioned, not to be understood, but definitely to be copied as soon as possible.

As the boy clatters down the rickety stairwell, Cecily leans back against a bookshelf and shuts her eyes. Her bones pulse with deep twinges; her chin and lip sting raw just from breathing on them.

"Cecily," she croaks, "is my name."

"Yes. I asked."

His face so close. He asked? Whom did he ask?

"I'm Beau."

He watches her eyes widen as she takes this in: she remembers her "Beau Geste" T-shirt at the Japanese restaurant. With a wicked grin he offers her tea, making her forget how mean he was to laugh at her like that.

Beau, the first syllable of beautiful. Was he as beautiful as she thought upon first seeing him? She scrutinizes him over her steaming tea. Hhmmm. Disconcerting that he stares right into her like that. Is he really so tall, or does she just feel smaller than usual? Sipping tea over her broken lip, she tries not to let the hot glass touch it.

"You'll make it swell up. Needs ice," and he reaches over and removes the glass from her hand. Lord! She wants to kiss him, stabbing pain in her lip and all.

When his face comes close to peer at her wounds, she has a view of him down her nose. Those black eyes sneaking into her dreams for so many weeks are an active and disconcerting force. Plus, his nose now comes into focus: it casts his face into that of an Afghan warlord. Just the kind of face she most admires.

Steam from the two hot teas swirls around them. Drifting, Cecily pictures this man with a feathered headdress streaming behind and a lance covered with ancient carvings. She sees him in a homespun doublet and loose linen shirt wet with sweat and gray with smoke. She can put him into the robe and armor of one carrying Mithras to Britain, standing alone among old stones at full moon, and then at the prow of a long boat in an ice-studded sea, his helmet horned and burnished and a fur cloak open at his throat because he revels in the cold, and Cecily definitely sees him, feels him, lounging on the verandah in a big cane chair, staring across green Delta rolling down to the river while young ladies chatter softly in his ear, calling, Beau, Beau, Beau...

"I'll call you Cecil. Don't like Cecily."

She jumps, startled from her fantasies. Focusing, she observes Beau's face change very little as he speaks. She finds this unnervingly sexy. What's even stranger, Beau has Wellington's nickname and Beau wears Wellington's nose, and Beau certainly looks as heroic, more heroic, than she imagined possible. She says as if in a dream, as if said by someone else, "I'm married."

"Yes. I asked."

Yes, she wants to be on those ships taking the roll and swell held against him, and yes, she wants him to look up amid lighting his cheroot as she descends that long curved staircase, and she wants to be oiled and draped and dragged to the sultan's bed, to feel his hand under her chin and be forced to look up to meet her fate. She can tell he feels the same.

Cecily is dizzy with her rushing thoughts, all these bizarre images from a lifetime of romantic notions converging and bombarding her. The pressure builds until she finally blurts, "Beau, let's — oh, this is crazy!"

He watches her expectantly. He seems to know what she will say before she does. Heart pounding, she rushes out, "Beau, have you been to Everest? Have you?"

He holds the glass in his hands and rolls it back and forth as if to warm himself. He leans over and brushes her cheek with his lips, avoiding her wounds with the softest most seductive kisses she can imagine. She shivers.

"Not yet, Cecil." Then he states with finality, "We will go together, we will walk to Lhasa, if you want." And he nods, "It is meant."

"Oh, Beau!"

He sits up, suddenly all business.

"But first, let's eat. You hungry?"

"Starved."

And she is. Ravenous.

20

THEY SIT IN A TIBETAN RESTAURANT she has never noticed before, mostly because it is such a hovel. Tattered carpets hang on the walls and none too clean cloths cover the tables. Cecily toys with greasy chow mein, which arrives long before the *momos*. She certainly hopes the cooks use different oil for the *momos* — but of course that doesn't matter, does it? It's not important. At this very moment, Cecily reminds herself, she wouldn't care if the *momos* never arrive.

This man who calls himself Beau is like no one she ever thought to meet, but not because she has never wanted to meet someone, some man like him. She just never believed someone, some man like Beau, would want to meet her.

After years of civil, chivalrous men with studied manners and veiled eyes, Beau's directness takes her out of being Cecily Havenshack, diplomat's spouse. Where this leaves her isn't clear yet. She does know this: he will move her. He will cause movement in her life. She has known from the beginning he will cause an earthquake in her very still, very perfect life.

Perhaps that's why she doesn't want to tell him anything personal. She might want to keep from him any information he could use as a weapon, although why she's still sitting here with thoughts like these, she doesn't know. It's not like her at all.

With this in mind, she sits here observing Beau, who is watching Cecily of the soft brown skin and unruly hair, split lip and scraped chin. Lounging back in his chair, he is the most provocative man in the world. She was wrong about his being so tall. It is only that his broad shoulders and the way he holds his head and, well, that way he has of looking down his nose gives an impression of great height.

Flustered, she tugs at her blouse. The soft material is still stretched out from Beau's fist. She pauses on the odd thought that hitting him again really hard would be as thrilling as kissing him. She smiles. Just this causes her lip to begin dripping blood. Embarrassed, she tries to hide her chin with her hand.

Beau's eyes narrow. He remonstrates, "Don't."

Distracted by the blood on her face, she doesn't notice Beau's swift change of mood. She has shifted her eyes from his a second too soon.

Pretending to be resting her chin on her hand, she looks for a waiter. My god, the wound feels like a canyon.

Another thought strikes her, a sudden social panic at the thought of someone she knows seeing her all bloody like this. In a tone that eludes her, Beau repeats, "I said don't, Cecil."

She is deaf to the change in him. So, Beau reaches across the table and pulls her wrist out from under her chin. Hard, so it hurts. She tries to retrieve her arm, but he holds her a little too firmly without any apparent effort.

In her astonishment, Cecily recognizes that she is again very afraid of this man. She regrets deciding to have dinner with him and tries to pull free, only to be squeezed even tighter.

Gasping, "Let go!"

Beau hisses, "You gonna do what I say?"

Her voice rises, "Let go! Beau!"

He continues to squeeze.

"Beau, I'm not used to — *oww!*"

Peoples' heads turn. He nods to her like all is normal, then murmurs, "My little flower," and he turns over the inside of her wrist and kisses it.

Cecily flushes from her scalp to her toes, a furnace. Sipping her tea to calm down, she watches this contradictory man return to the chow mein. He is again so, so polite. She begins to distrust her own senses. She holds her right wrist lightly in her lap. Moving it causes twinges that grow more painful by the moment. Glancing down, she sees her wrist is swollen and turning deep bruise-red.

It is then that she stops sticking bandaids on her misgivings and admits that all rationalizations for his behavior are possibly futile, probably futile. He is a runaway train, and she had better be really careful here.

"Cecil."

She looks up, pulled out of her uneasy thoughts. The light is soft on his face. His eyes call out to her to — what? Save him? Love him? Hold him close after he kills someone? But Cecily melts again, the protesting part of her going down first.

She might come to like the name Cecil. It does have more corners to it. Cecily has always sounded so girlish, and people are always charmed by the name, then by her big green eyes and her fuzzy hair, and by not knowing exactly which race she belongs to. Cecil. Yes, a name with more muscle.

She whispers, "Yes, Beau?"

"I'm broke tonight, you gotta pay the bill."

She blinks. Broke? He has no money to pay for chow mein and *momos* on a chipped plate in a third-rate restaurant in this city? He is kidding.

No, he is obviously not kidding. Cecily blinks again. No one has no money. No Westerner, anyway. Even the Freaks have money, kroners and liras, money like that.

She looks down at her wrist, which throbs when she makes the merest move. "Yes, of course. How much?"

He scrutinizes her sitting so tight and offended across the table, and he laughs scornfully, reaches over and grabs her hand, her left hand, and pulls it to his lips. When she flinches, he smiles slowly, penetrating her belly with a voluptuous twist of his lips. She draws in a ragged breath.

He murmurs, "Cecil, Cecil. No harm! No harm. Sit up, make you taller."

She straightens. He signals a waiter and orders the bill in what sounds like perfect Nepali, then turns back to her. Beau sits staring at her. She holds her right wrist in her left hand and sits as still as she possibly can.

Beau gnaws on a toothpick and leans back in his chair. He says nothing, shares nothing, asks nothing. The silence extends to a point Cecily considers almost spooky, especially with him staring at her that way. She searches for something to say, a question to ask.

"So Beau, uh, where did you go to school?"

He removes the toothpick. He doesn't answer right away, and Cecily swallows anxiously. Beau finally says, "New Orleans."

Why is he looking at her like that? She rushes in, "Oh? Really? Did you go to Tulane?"

She feels him withdraw even more, his eyes doing that flat thing again. She desperately tries to remember another school in New Orleans. "Or, or, Auburn?"

No, that isn't in New Orleans, it's somewhere else. Beau is now coldly silent. Cecily looks around the restaurant, jerking out, "Gee, I wonder where that waiter is."

She holds her right wrist gently in her left palm, hidden below the height of the table. Beau growls, "I stayed one day and realized college is a fucking wasteland for fucking losers."

"Oh," she answers faintly, her left hand to her neck, and she looks again for the bloody waiter, thinking, Not go to college? No one she knows has not gone to college. Everyone goes to college, don't they? Well, except for marines and, and, well, mechanic-type guys. Everyone else she knows went on to at least junior college or art school or something, because of course they knew they would become more successful and make more money — oh. That's right. No money.

"I decided it was a pile of shit. Four years of piss-pure shit."

She thinks then that something else may have been wrong. Like his not getting accepted. Or that he didn't get a scholarship; after all, he has no money now so maybe he's never had any. Can he read, she wonders? His stare continues unrelentingly hostile from across the table.

She feels suddenly exhausted. The food has found uneasy shelter in her belly. She aches all over. Craving a tub full of hot water and a glass of wine, all she wants is to soak with her eyes closed. Well, a full tub isn't possible because the water heater won't heat that much at a time. Still, half-full would do under the circumstances. She brightens when she spies the waiter.

"Here he comes!" she says a little too loudly. Moving to pull her bag from off the back of her chair, she uses the wrong hand and cringes in sudden agony.

Avoiding Beau's eyes, Cecily bends over her Chinese silk coin-purse with its tasseled drawstrings and delicate embroidery and counts out the rupees. When she gives the money to the waiter, she realizes Beau is still staring coldly at her from across the table, the toothpick rolling back and forth between his thumb and fingers. She draws tight the purse strings and stuffs it into her bag. Gathering together all her forces, she looks Beau in the eyes.

"Well. I must be going now."

He does not even blink. She hesitates, then states firmly, "I have a mahjong game in Patan. In twenty minutes! I just remembered." She clears her throat, "They would never forgive me if I were late." Doesn't he ever need to blink? "So I must go now."

He still hasn't budged, and is eyeing her steadily. She is quelled. She feels spineless.

"You're a fucking snob, Cecil."

She drops her good hand from her throat. She straightens, looks down her nose, pursing her lips and raising her brow.

"I? A snob? I'm no snob, Beau."

She stands. He doesn't. He repeats, "You're a fucking snob."

"I'm not!" She clears her throat, cursing herself for squeaking. "I'm not a snob. That's absurd."

He remains lounging in his chair and twirling his toothpick. His accusation has given her some much-needed backbone. She nods like Queen Victoria, "I really must be going." She pauses. "May I drop you — somewhere?"

He does not answer. She stands with her bag clutched before her, keeping her spine stiff. "Well, I'm not a snob, I assure you!"

Beau insolently shrugs one shoulder. She is on the edge of tears. Hastily, she moves from the table, saying, "I must go. Goodbye, Beau, it's —" she gulps. And he, the ass! sits there mocking her. She continues, "It's been interesting. Painfully interesting."

She turns and walks toward the door. Behind her, he says just loud enough for her to hear, "I'll see you soon, Cecil."

She keeps herself from glancing back. Was that a threat? Cecily shivers convulsively as she pushes open the door and feels moist night air brush over her like a washcloth wiping away mud.

21

INSIDE A HALF-FILLED TUB with a half-empty wineglass, Cecily holds a wash cloth to her lip. She's half-wrinkled from lying half-submerged. At first the small but numerous injuries burn like hellfire, but this eventually subsides to a milder discomfort. Her bruised, swollen wrist, however, is unfortunate. It's possibly just cracked and not broken because her fingers do move. She can't believe the pain. She can do nothing with her right hand except lay it limp across her wet belly.

It is tiresome that Beau's face appears in the very air at the merest thought of him. Marble tiles multiply his image like a carnival mirror. When she moves, he even ripples across the bath water. She shuts her eyes. She opens one cautiously, then her pulse hammers — *my god!* she thinks, Beau's eyes moved!

But no? No. She did not see that. Did she? Cecily wills the marble tiles blank. Goosebumps rise and move across her brown belly and floating nipples. Glaring at the tiles, she finds them again blank marble. She sighs, then settles down farther into her bath and reaches for her wine.

As her fingers close around the glass, a flicker of movement in the wall tiles causes her to spasm, knocking the wine into the tub. She bolts up, scrambles for a towel with her left hand, then steps out of the tub while carefully keeping her back to the wall. Her one-handed attempts at drying off are awkward and inefficient. A sudden thought distracts her and she stops toweling, her hair still dripping.

So why did his never going to college bother her so much? Just because she went to college, and just because everyone she knows went to college — that is, everyone she has ever been friends with, certainly they all went.

Thinking back on it, not everyone from her graduating class went on to college. Those in her home town who were from neighborhoods down near the factories, a lot of those kids didn't do much after high school except go to work in those very factories and buy new cars and stay there forever. Nothing except earn their own livings, set their own schedules, control their own daily lives. She squelches an old envy. No, those kids didn't go on to college like her and everyone else she ever knew personally.

Perhaps there were ones like herself, the dutiful, the well-fed and outfit-coordinated, who didn't go on to college. Could be. She doesn't remember any. Thinking back, those who didn't go on to college generally seemed just as intelligent as she. Maybe not good students, but smart in lots of different ways from her own way.

She also knows that many of those same students who never went to college were the ones who frightened her with their harsh wit. They scared her with their abrupt emotions and their brusque laughter. They took risks she avoided vigilantly. With snorts and with dismissive glances, they slouched and sneered through each class, defiantly not preparing for college.

Is this why Beau's lack of at least a bachelor's degree bothers her so much, because he is that bitter, slouching type? He is, isn't he. The type who will say things she'd rather not hear once in her whole life and do things she would never ever do.

She drops the towel and unscrews lotion, squeezing some onto her breasts, slowly rubbing it in. She reaches for powder and liberally dusts her shoulders and tummy and between her legs, all without the help of her right hand. Keeping her backside to the wall, she prepares another compress for her throbbing lip and burning chin. She stands holding it to her face with her left hand, thinking.

One difference is, if Beau had gone to college and still turned out this way, then his eccentric behavior would be the result of too much education. Well-informed anger just doesn't seem as scary to her. She can name lots of bitter lawyers and moody doctors. Even her father, a very well-educated realtor, was often safely furious over events he couldn't possibly change, so she does know about educated anger.

Thinking again of those horrible-wonderful high school years, she realizes those classmates who were aglow with rage were having lives unlike hers. It's as if they pulled up their personalities in a bucket from a tainted well, and they always seemed most angry at people like herself. Certainly a number of those high school classmates disliked her intensely. She shudders at a particularly ugly memory.

Trying to bend her right wrist, Cecily whimpers. She nods to her reflection: yes, Beau is the way he is from forever. He is bad bad bad for her, and she must do her very best to avoid him.

Innumerable ice packs later, she gets her wrist to bend.

22

LATER THE SAME NIGHT, a hammering noise enters Cecily's dream, alters it, ends it. This sound finally wakens her. Once she rubs the sleep from her eyes and sits up, she can also hear shouting.

Curiosity finally overcoming fear, she gets out of bed, wrapping the top sheet like a toga. She peers out the closest window into a rose garden below. No one out there. The night drowses quietly on this side of the palace. It must be some problem at that house on the far side of the rice field. They must be having another of their family arguments.

Then she remembers that her Italian neighbors are back in Rome for monsoon. If the noise does indeed come from their house, wouldn't their *chokidar* stop it? Perhaps their *chokidar* is hiding in his quarters. Perhaps hers is. Oh dear, oh dear. Suddenly, silence. She listens on tiptoe and hears nothing. Perhaps it was a street fight, after all, now over. She can maybe go back to bed.

Before unwrapping the sheet and crawling back through the mosquito net, French shutters wide open onto a cool and cloudy night, Cecily once more listens carefully. Nothing. She crawls back into bed, snuggling down under the antique comforter.

Less than five seconds later the ruckus begins again. Her eyes snap open. She stares up through the netting. It has to be the Italian consul's staff. Being neighborly ends here and now, except she really doesn't want to go over and deal with a possible drunk person. She pulls the quilt over her head, which muffles the noise, but not completely. She can almost feel vibrations from the pounding.

In a burst of outraged energy, she throws off the comforter and rolls out of bed, retrieving her sheet from the floor and wrapping it under her arms. She opens the immense old door of her bedroom and marches out to do her duty, sheet trailing, then abruptly stops and backs up against the door, pressing into the wood frame.

All that pounding and shouting is not next door, it is right here at her own palace! Probably at her own front door and just muffled by the rooms in between.

Knees knocking, she leans on the door frame and clutches her throat. She listens. A fire? Someone run over by a Tata truck? Or, my god, the long overdue revolution, finally beginning in her yard?

Still, upon listening more carefully, the voice doesn't sound driven by fear or even pain. Listening closer, it sounds like only one mad person.

She has a dreadful thought: oh no. No. It is not conceivable that the person at her front door is who she thinks it is.

She edges away from her bedroom and down the long hall, her left hand still clutching her throat. As she creeps along past one room, then another, she doesn't bother to turn on the lights, preferring for the first time in her life to move in inky darkness.

The cacophony grows as Cecily approaches the front hall. There, she is reluctant to enter the foyer itself, where the noise is distorted by echoes. After gathering her courage, she calls in a cracking voice, "Who is it?" The pounding stops. Silence is worse.

She licks her dry lips and hoarsely calls, "What do you want?"

Silence grows loud after all the noise. Christ! Why doesn't he answer? And where the hell is her *chokidar!*

"Shiva? Shiva! Come here!"

Her cry travels backward through the emptiness of her palace, but Cecily doubts her cry will reach past the man on her front steps, much less down the drive to the gatehouse and the probably well-hidden Shiva. She places her left hand on the wall for support as someone outside the door moves, the shadows changing.

"Shiva!" This time her voice goes high.

The shadow growls, "He's not here."

His words travel through solid matter with no effort. He is perfectly understandable now that the pounding has stopped. She tries to speak, squeaks, clears her throat, tries again. "Who—?"

For a moment, silence. Then, "Beau, Cecil. It's Beau."

How did he discover where she lives?

"Open up, Cecil. It's Beau."

Open up? Is he crazy? "Beau? What do you want?"

There is no ready answer from his side of the door. Then, "I want to talk to you."

To talk? To talk? She squeaks, "Why?"

She stops her left hand from wringing her own throat and stands up straighter. She must calm herself, she must not be so frightened. That's how awful things happen, one person panics and pulls the other one into it. She takes some deep breaths to steady herself, asking, "Where's Shiva? What have you done with my *chokidar!*"

When he answers, Beau sounds exasperated. "I don't know! I don't care about your damn *chokidar!*"

It occurs to her that perhaps it really is Shiva's night off.

"Wh-what do you want?"

Though stuttering, her voice is now under better control, not shrieking all over the room.

"Why are you here?"

"Cecil, let me in!"

"How did you find out where I live?"

"Cecil, I'm telling you! Let me in!"

Let him in? Is he insane? After beating on her door and shouting crazy stuff in the middle of the night, he thinks she should let him in? What does he want from her?

"What do you want from me?"

No response. She watches his shadow on the glass doors. He stiffens, drawing himself up taller. His shadow looms threateningly. How can she get rid of him?

"Is there something you, uh, that you want—"

He hits the door once, hard. Five-centimeter-thick wood cracks. Cecily jumps farther back and crouches against the wall. Then, his shadow abruptly twists and disappears.

After a long time, she rises. Is he gone?

"Beau?" He seems gone. "Beau?"

But still she doesn't move toward the door to make sure.

Finally, she retreats and trudges back down the hall and through many rooms, turning on lights as she goes. The night is by now half over. She will stay up for the rest of it and ponder this event. What could Beau have wanted?

She shivers again. She flicks on the kitchen light, her fingers remaining on the knob and her eyes moving up above the door: yes, the doorbell is still connected. Well! He could have damn well used the doorbell instead of pounding and shouting and scaring her. Rude and stupid. The bloody uneducated twit.

23

CECILY SPENDS THE REST of that night in her kitchen sitting on a high stool, drinking tea and reading *The Rising Nepal* at one end of a huge old table scarred since the nineteenth century. Sunrise comes earlier than she expects. Summer's shortest night passed several weeks ago, but the mornings continue as dewily early, the evenings as lingeringly long.

Stretching, she stands and unwinds the towel from her hair, still wet from a pre-sunrise wash. Fluffing curls, she saunters out of the kitchen, leaving her dishes and coffeepot on the table, the newspaper scattered on the floor, the towel on Cook's stool. She also leaves the lights on even though daylight has settled everywhere.

Suddenly, she remembers an engagement scheduled for later this morning, a surprise baby shower and brunch for a pregnant friend. Her calendar has remained so blank all summer that she finds herself for once looking forward to a party. Besides, she has always enjoyed the silly games played for sillier prizes at showers, they are just plain fun. She walks happily into her bedroom to polish her twenty nails.

She sits on a cushion on the floor before an antique French vanity, possibly one from the Sun King's personal collection. With one knee up under her chin, she peers over it inspecting her toenails. She works slowly with her left hand, toe by toe, perfection important. As they dry, she lies back flat on the floor with the cushion still under her bottom. She points her chin up, stretching, observing the mosquito net hanging from its high frame above the bed behind her. Maybe she should get some ribbons to catch up the netting during the day.

Straightening her neck, Cecily raises her legs and inspects her toes painted a nice glossy peach that looks great against her brown skin. Fingernails take longer because she has to dry the right hand before beginning the left. When she tries to hold the brush with her bruised right hand and paint her left nails, she winces in serious discomfort.

Cecily's threshold for pain has never been high: putting on nail polish for a baby shower does not seem a good enough reason to raise her tolerance, so she carefully rubs off the color dried upon her right hand, then pads down her private hall to the bathroom where she rummages in a deep cabinet till she finds a bottle of apricot lotion. As she passes back to the bedroom, she glances at a grandfather clock hulking between two open French windows: there's an hour to get ready and arrive before the guest of honor, whom she absolutely has to precede because of the fun of the surprise. Plenty of time.

Slipping into a peach-colored sundress that buttons to her waist from the V of its neckline, she shakes it straight and puts her hands into deep pockets. She groans, must be more careful with that wrist. Now, should she wear a slip? No, too hot. Looking through shelves and drawers for that thin leather belt, she also finds a lost trove of silk scarves. Pulling them out to spill across the bedspread, she spies one with a hint of peach glowing through the abstract browns. She shakes it out, placing the silk scarf around her neck so it hangs down the front of her dress. Perfection.

Again at the vanity, she unhooks the hinges of her Kenya-made jewelry box and assesses her collection. Finally she decides on a pair of gold hoops she had made the last time she went to Bangkok.

She opens another closet and rummages around for a favorite pair of Italian leather thongs and slides them on. Awkwardly brushing her hair with her left hand, she remembers that she owns an extra wide bracelet that would easily cover her bruised wrist. She digs out the hinged jade bangle that fits snug like a cuff and double checks its tiny latch, which is shaped like Pegasus. Stewart bought it for her that first time they traveled in Greece, so long ago in so many ways, but she still likes the bracelet. It feels surprisingly cool around her sore wrist.

Now, ready? Dress, scarf, shoes, belt, the merest hint of jewelry. Anything else? Oh yes, present for baby. And her bag, where is her bag? She locates her straw bag, fills it with the present plus other vital items and slings it over her shoulder, feeling for the palace keys through the straw as she walks out of her bedroom, thinking, if traffic isn't too bad, she'll stop to see if that poster shop is open. After all, Sunday is really Monday here so it should be open, and suddenly she wants to buy a Krishna print right now, for no reason she can fathom.

So, Cecily is occupied with deep thoughts as she walks out the door and locks it, paying no attention to the dozens of windows left wide open. She drops the keys back in her purse as she steps off the porch into the porte cochère and then looks up.

Odd, there is already a taxi parked in the porte cochère. Why would a taxi be parked here? The gate is still locked, and now the driver is looking at her kind of funny. Why is this?

It never occurs to her to look around and find Beau standing on the other side of the trellis.

When he says, "Cecil," she whirls and pales. Then, sheepish in her sudden fear, Cecily shakily holds her ground. Has Beau been waiting for her all night? Patiently and quietly waiting for hours?

She has no recourse except to face up to him, lifting her quivering chin. "Oh! Beau."

"Good morning, Cecil."

She swallows at his tone. "Yes. I mean, uh, good morning."

She swallows again, continues, "Look, hm? I would love to stay and talk with you, but, really I can't right now, I have this baby shower to go to. So..." Cecily tries to cock a rueful brow.

"I've already got a taxi."

"Oh? A taxi? Well, hm, yes. Thanks anyway, but I thought I'd just —"

"I'll help you get in." He grips her elbow and propels her forcefully toward the taxi.

"But, Beau! I really have to be somewhere else, it's a surprise, you see, so I can't just not show up early!"

She babbles. She tries resisting. She begins to struggle, yelling now, "No! Really! I have nothing to say to you!"

Then, horrified, "I'm *not* getting in that taxi with you! Beau! Help! Help!"

He lowers his hand to her jade bangle and presses his fingers around her wrist, and she turns paper-white and shuts up because she can't do anything else. When he pulls her toward the taxi, she follows stumbling.

"It's all right, Cecil, you're going to listen while I explain some things."

He pushes her into the taxi, shuts the door, and walks around to the other side. She twists around, eyes locked involuntarily upon him, compulsively fascinated, making no attempt to flee. Beau slides in close beside her and shuts the door.

"*Budhanilkantha ma jaane,*" he orders. They start down the long driveway and out the gate, and absolutely no one at all has noticed any of this. As they accelerate down the street, they sit in silence. She feels him shift slightly and she startles, but he does not touch her.

Cecily can no longer stand the silence and demands an explanation in a voice like a bad oboe.

"You can't be serious! This can't be serious, Beau!"

To his mute stare she repeats, "You just can't," but it sounds weaker and ineffective even to her ears.

So next she orders the driver to stop in English because she can't remember any Nepali. But the driver ignores her after a curt command from Beau. The driver actually laughs.

Cecily sinks back into her corner, frustrated and nervous and now more afraid than before, a truly toxic blend of response and reality.

They curve onto Ring Road and head north. On and on they drive without seeing anyone who could stop this taxi and make Beau let her out. As they approach the first turnoff, slowing to avoid cows on the road, she gloomily considers jumpings out — hey wait, that's a solution! She thinks desperately, trying to decide. Her left hand steals to the door.

Jumping will be extremely dangerous. But staying in this taxi with this unpredictable man seems more perilous over the long course, so she prepares herself, watching him out the corner of her eye as they slow and swing out around those cows. Almost, almost, almost — but then the driver does not slow down enough that she feels she could jump and live.

And not only does she want to live, she also needs to be able to run. Slowly she withdraws her left hand from the door and drops it back down beside her on the seat and tries to untense her body. But mounting fear of this taxi's destination, where Beau is planning who knows what, has driven Cecily into a panic loop.

She attempts rational thought. What is it that Stew told her? What did they learn in those required terrorist classes at the embassy? Upon being taken hostage, what is most important is to keep the mind clear, keep the senses acute. Hmm, that's not good. Except for true astonishment and a distinctively ominous churning of her gut, Cecily's senses are now shut down tight. They're huddling in self-protection behind a very frightened epidermis. And her legs are clamped so tight to the floor, she will break in half if she tries jumping out of this taxi.

Beau lounges next to her. He appears lost in contemplation of passing rice fields. She watches his profile from behind lowered lashes as they speed on.

Soon, another intersection approaches, and Cecily realizes it is now or never. She also realizes she won't be able to do it at all if she gives much more thought to the act of jumping out of a moving car. Does this make her a coward? She must decide if she is more afraid of speeding into concrete than of staying in this taxi with Beau.

Distance disappears between the taxi and the turnoff to Budhanilkantha. Closing, close, nearly there. Is Beau watching? She carefully eyes him. No.

A crowd of children, bless them! wanders out into the road, causing the driver to break his speed. Again she glances at Beau. She lets her left hand slip up to the door handle. Luckily for her he isn't paying attention now that he thinks he has her.

Closer, closer. A few seconds more, a few meters more. Is he watching? Is he! No. Not watching, almost almost, slower, damn it! almost — now!

"Don't do it, Cecil."

Beau slides his fingers under her jade bangle, pressing cruelly into the damaged flesh. She gasps and jerks back from the door, missing her last opportunity to open it and jump out. Now they will turn onto the long stretch up to Budhanilkantha that has no junctions and is on a raised dike, and there will be no reasons for the driver to slow down.

She watches lush green rice fields go by with a fatalistic calm. She glances down at her watch to see if she can possibly still make it to the baby shower before it ends, after this creature finishes torturing her or whatever it is he has in mind, and she discovers she forgot to strap it to her wrist. Thinking about it, she can't even remember when she last saw the watch. Great. Along with everything else, she has succeeded in misplacing time.

Back to watching terraced fields, she asks herself, why Budhanilkantha? That's kilometers up to the northernmost part of the valley. Budhanilkantha sits as far north as one can go in the valley and not start up the side of a foothill toward Everest. She becomes very still for a moment, then shakes off a premonition crawling up her neck.

Beau shifts on the seat beside her. She vows not to give him the satisfaction of a glance or a flinch. To occupy her quaking mind, she sets her bag on her lap and stares inside, the two big rings flopping apart and gaping open. Inside lie various items, none of which look much like a weapon, which is what Cecily feels she definitely needs. She digs around with her left hand and comes up with a book of matches. Could she set him on fire? She fiddles with them, considering this possibility. Then she drops them back into the pile and fumbles on through the contents.

Resolutely she concentrates on the items inside the bag: brush, sunglasses, keys and bandana; a miniature leather note pad; assorted pens and pencils, old notes and lists; a library card — wait!

Something slips out from inside the note pad. A penknife. Yes! Hallelujah, this is it. She can stab him! Shallowly, true, but it will still hurt. And she very much wants to hurt Beau.

She thinks maybe she has been too obvious about the penknife, so she continues fumbling through her bag but pays no real attention to what she touches. How to get the knife out? She has it in her left hand, the one away from Beau. After a moment's consideration, she chooses the bandana. She lifts her right hand and carefully reaches in and pulls out the piece of cloth.

She begins lightly flapping it at her face, pretending to wave away the driver's cigarette smoke, and valiantly pretending the pain of doing this with her abused wrist isn't bringing tears to her eyes. A moan of pain is disguised as a cough. Beau merely glances at her, then stares back out his window.

Her wrist growing unbearable, Cecily bends and slips her purse back to the floor. When she lets go and sits back up she still has the penknife in her left palm. After a few more flaps, she drops the cloth on her lap and looks out the window, letting her eyes and cheeks dry. Rice fields are below the rutted road now as they bump up a ridge that eventually becomes one of the spines up mighty Shivapuri. Feeling enough time has passed, and now somewhat more calm and collected, she slowly and carefully brings her palmed knife up to her lap and wraps her hand in the bandana. She unwraps it, wraps it and fiddles for a few moments, letting her tension loose in these small gestures.

When she has the penknife sufficiently twined into the fabric, she sits still and counts to twenty, then moves the bandana to her left pocket. As she stuffs it in, and he makes no move to stop her nor indicates he has noticed anything amiss, Cecily feels buoyant, a lifting of the dread hanging low since she heard Beau's voice behind her after closing the front door of the palace.

What damage, if any, she can possibly do with a penknife is negligible. But if she can hurt him even a little, she will feel better.

Having a secret weapon breeds the tiniest bit of confidence, which blooms to anger at her abductor. She's missed her surprise baby shower for sure; they are almost to the edge of Budhanilkantha, and now she'll never get back in time.

Cecily renews her demand to know where the hell they're going and what the hell he thinks he's doing. Beau squeezes her thigh till she cries out and tries to peel his hand off. This distracts her from every other intent, and she sucks air like a cartoon when he finally lets go.

As they slow to enter the village, Beau wraps his arm around Cecily's shoulder, pulling her to him with a jerk. She stiffens, anticipating more pain. None comes, but with his one arm around her and the other holding her leg, she is prevented from moving.

Not for the first time this morning does fear wash over her, lapping at her reason. Beau's closeness reminds her of a possibility she has not yet considered: Is he planning to kill her? Out here in the mountains where only he and the taxi driver will know?

She searches frantically for help from any quarter, her mind racing. Anna! Her best friend will miss her at the party, surely! But then, truthfully, there really is no reason for Anna to question Cecily's absence from a baby shower, everyone is too used to Kathmandu no-shows and monsoon hermits.

Her employees? Preema was off, and the rest of the staff would never question her comings and goings, at least they never have. She glumly admits it will take a long time for anyone to realize she is missing, and then even longer to decide what to do about it.

Oh. My. God. Cecily shudders convulsively. Beau, tightening his hold, murmurs soft words she can't understand through the sudden roaring in her head. He sits so close, his face next to hers, that she can't turn to watch his mouth or else their lips will touch. Cecily leans away, closing her eyes. His grip upon her tightens.

She mustn't give in. She must remain calm, she must calm herself. Her only weapon, that little penknife wrapped in a bandana deep inside her pocket, seems truly meager.

24

SUN BEATS DOWN on the mountainside, hardening mud from last night's rain. Kathmandu sits on the valley's floor far below to the south. Despite the heat, despite Beau's arm tight around her, Cecily shivers as they watch the taxi bump downhill toward town with Cecily's straw bag in the trunk. Any hope of escape grows increasingly faint.

The driver took them up this abysmal track until he could force the vehicle no farther. All the children who chased the taxi through Budhanilkantha are now far behind. She and Beau stand halfway up Shivapuri, watching the very well-paid driver head back down to Kathmandu after a short conference in Nepali with Beau.

Cecily fights a need to shriek at the heavens. So far all the gods are deaf today. She attempts standing there all cool and centered like she knows Anna would, sort of flippant-calm, her hands tight in the pockets of the sundress which is draping perfectly about her calves.

Beau's backpack sits at his feet. For the first time she notices he's wearing a military shirt with camouflage trousers. Even worse, she cannot see his eyes through his mirrored sunglasses, she can only see herself. Through all the chaos of her fears, she hears Beau explain that they will be out here seven days. Through that roaring in her head, she understands finally what he is saying about a trek he's planned for just the two of them. All alone together.

In a monotone, he continues explaining how the taxi will pick them up on the seventh day at some village far to the east of Kathmandu Valley, somewhere out on the road up to the Chinese border, and between now and then they will be trekking on this particular trail, sort of come sideways at Helambu's main trail, head up and back down, and then they'll find that village to the east and meet the driver. Just like that. His seriousness penetrates Cecily's growing panic.

Seven days? Trekking for seven days? He must be joking. He has to be joking. She looks down at her outfit so carefully selected for the baby shower. She doesn't even have real shoes on.

Her fears turn to anger. Well! If he wants her to move from this spot, he'll bloody well have to carry her! What was he thinking! She wedges her painted toenails farther into Italian soles and scowls at herself in his sunglasses.

Fury giving her clarity, Cecily remembers her idiotic fantasies of him as a savior prince of the universe. Had she temporarily lost her senses? Ha! She realizes now he is absolutely a toad, never a prince! Never has been and never will be a prince of any sort, and in fact, he is actually a wart on that toad's ass! She fists her hands and widens her stance, glaring at him.

He finally growls, "Cecil, I realize I gave you no warning." He clears his throat, "and I've got a feeling you won't be happy about this, but I, we, I mean," he compresses his lips, then continues, "we are going to trek. You and me, like we talked." Cecily is not admitting to any such agreement.

In a change of mood, Beau shifts restlessly, finally blurting, "Well, shit! You're pissed, I know!" He continues more softly, "It's just that I've got to be alone with you, Cecil."

If he thought this would elicit capitulation, he was dead wrong. Cecily yells, "How in hell did you think up such a wonderful plan! My god, Beau. My god my god my god!"

He has no response. Her injured sensibilities gaining strength, she inquires, "You're making me go on some trek? Dressed like this?" She shakes the skirt of her summer frock at him and flaps one leather thong. "You moron!"

Now that his friendly moment is over, Beau is again iron on the move. "Well, if you can talk, you can walk. One way or another you, Cecil, are going to Helambu!" Beau reaches for her.

Sudden as his movement is, Cecily moves faster. She steps backwards up the slope out of Beau's reach. He glares at her with his hand clenching on air. She hisses, "Touch me and I'll vomit!"

Beau shrugs. He bends to pick up the backpack. It is when he's bent over that she strikes out with her foot in a kick that catches Beau off balance and tips him over on his back in a slide down the hill.

She meant for him to fall the other way, more toward a nearby ravine, but he slides in the direction she wants to go. She takes off anyway, skidding around him and angling back toward the path beyond. Beau struggles to stop himself and stand, but he slips again, giving Cecily a bit more head start. She laughs wildly.

Then she also begins a slide, another little avalanche, scraping along on one leg as she goes down the path and slithers through mud, and she loses the few meters she's gained. Beau rolls over in a somersault that brings him up against her with a whack — something she has seen parachutists do, which frightens her even more to think he knows such things — and he grabs her arm, pulling her up short. She pulls the other way as hard as she can, throwing him off balance again. He follows her down the path in a tumble that leaves them slowly bumping to a halt.

She lies with her face smashed into the ground, feeling the cut of her lip moist in the dirt. It now has the company of other open wounds.

Beau slides off her back and flips her over, pinning her arms on either side of her face. His sunglasses have fallen off. Breathing raggedly and holding her flat, his nose one inch from hers, he states, "You are going to Helambu," emphasizing each word so Cecily will finally get it.

Of course she is going to Helambu. How can she refuse such an offer. Beau jerks her up and brushes her off, arranging her hair around her face, then he pulls out a hankie and a canteen and cleans her lip, her knees, her elbows, all bleeding. Her butt is just bruised.

Cecily stands there defeated. She is going to Helambu or to wherever. Ineffectively she flaps at the dirt on her not so pretty party dress.

25

NOW THAT SHE HAS DONE IT, Cecily can imagine few activities more unpleasant than climbing a steep, muddy mountain in the middle of a sticky, monsoon day. She has to stop every other minute on the south slope up Shivapuri with Beau right behind — to catch her breath, to untangle her dress, to secure a wayward slipper.

Cecily vows she will escape this mad expedition, but with Beau behind her prodding all the time she soon grows too flustered and out of breath to mark the landscape with her memory. He does say once, while she holds onto a bush and gasps, that she will find a rhythm soon, it will get easier. But she has not yet found it, and she looks forward to reaching the top of this mountain, no matter where it leads, because the other side will be downhill.

Sun burns her shoulders, arms, feet and face. Beau gives her water from a small canteen while he briskly rubs lotion on the red parts. As the afternoon progresses and they slowly approach the top of Shivapuri, they finally reach a forest where shade helps her recover some shreds of poise.

In the rare moments when she has her breath and can think, Cecily wonders what other surprises this crazed man has stored away in his tiny mind, if he even has a mind. She wonders where all the Nepalis are who supposedly live on the slopes of Shivapuri. Stewart has said more than once he cannot go anywhere on his treks without tripping over people. If this mountain kingdom is so overpopulated, then where are all those Nepalis when she needs them? Where are all those trekking world travelers? And where is the top of this bloody mountain?

She stops again and rubs sweat from her face. Beau is close behind her and blocking any retreat down the path. Bloody bastard. She silently curses him with every foul word that she has ever heard, and then she creates a few apt descriptions of his personality and body parts. She feels a prod at her lower back, and they continue their ascent. Seven days of this? Isn't any of it downhill?

At last, she can see sky through the trees ahead. That means the summit is just up there, thank all the gods. Beau's easy and even breathing comes just behind her. Anger at her own uncontrolled panting pushes Cecily rapidly up the last few meters of Shivapuri.

Abruptly she comes upon a large clearing, at least thirty meters across. It is such a relief to be on flat ground! Her burst of energy takes her across the open area to the far edge. She looks around gratefully, then realizes they still haven't reached the summit of Shivapuri, which keeps going up to the west. They have emerged at a point where the path crosses this open knoll, then curves around and drops down the other side of the ridge.

To the south, Kathmandu Valley can no longer be seen. To the north unfolds a vista dropping sharply down before leading far, far up to the greater Himalayan peaks only fifty kilometers away but now mostly hidden by monsoon clouds. Cecily would have caught her breath at the view before her, if she had any breath left to catch.

"You can rest here."

His voice just behind her, she jumps and stumbles forward and almost goes over the edge of the cliff. She would have fallen a hundred meters before hitting a ledge, but Beau pulls her back, steadies her, then stalks away leaving her alone to fight for composure. She is a fool. She will have to control herself better. This is dangerous terrain; being skittish will do her no good.

Sitting there on the edge of what seems the last flat place on earth, Cecily reviews her situation. It more than disturbs her, and she briefly contemplates jumping off. However, the scenery slowly takes over her gloomy thoughts and eases away her discomfort, leaving her more relaxed. More fatalistic. She is still aware of Beau close by, but if she looks at one spot way across on another looming, massive foothill, she can almost forget how and why she is here. Time passes, slowing her breath.

"Let's go, Cecil."

She startles, but safely this time. Her heart resumes its anxious pounding, but she stubbornly ignores her abductor. They have been here less time than she needs, she can't even stand yet.

"We're going. Now, Cecil."

At his tone she stands, bristling. "Don't call me that bloody name!"

He steps toward her. "I said, let's go. Cecil."

She goes.

They angle left on a path slanting across the north side of Shivapuri, not downhill, but at least it isn't uphill. At least there is that.

As they wind through a denser forest, she finds she can walk better on this path and doesn't have to look down so much. Upon looking up, she trips and almost falls flat. Beau suggests she remove her hands from her pockets (she hadn't realized they'd been jammed inside her dress) because it is a dangerous habit, she needs them for balance, needs to have them free and available. She follows his advice without comment. She finds it, damn his black eyes, to be correct.

Soon she enters a shock-compromised, meditative state as she plods silently through high altitude forest. Birds offer up late afternoon noise, a dozen distinct calls, she counts them. The sky continues miraculously monsoon free, four days now, she counts them. As time passes and their steady pace hypnotizes her, Cecily almost, not quite, forgets why she is hiking through this forest. Walking on level ground and counting her steps helps this a lot.

Shadows are long before Beau orders her to halt. Sitting on a monsoon saturated log while he walks ahead a ways, out of sight after a moment, she makes no attempt to escape. It is just too far back now, and anyway he immediately returns. He gestures for her to get up, and she follows him down the path for another fifty meters before he suddenly turns left and surges up into the forest.

Cecily halts, dismayed at the thought of stepping off this trail into the woods, where there could be bears and snakes. Why can't they continue to follow this nice flat path? She shakes her head at Beau, who is holding out his hand to help her up over the first bit. He gestures impatiently, but she refuses, beginning to stumble backwards up the trail.

He steps back onto the path and reaches for her. She looks around desperately. Maybe she will run after all, she thinks, but her arm is held tight, and they move together up off the path through the tangled bushes, straight up the back side of Shivapuri.

After their initial plunge, she finds there isn't much undergrowth after all, but she keeps a fearful eye out for creepy-crawlies while Beau keeps his hand firmly on her arm. They slog maybe three minutes uphill, Cecily desperate for oxygen, before they enter a clearing.

Concentrating so hard on keeping up with his pace, she doesn't hear the rush of a stream. Finally looking around, Cecily freezes. In a moment of disorientation, she imagines she's in a glade she and Stewart found on a hike during that first vacation in Greece. She turns around in confusion, half expecting to see a tumble-down temple with red poppies growing inside. She then remembers that after they dallied in that Grecian glade, Stewart gave her the very jade bracelet she's wearing now.

Beau takes off his pack, setting it on a large rock.

"We stay here tonight." He turns and surveys the clearing with satisfaction.

She protests, "No!" Cecily's knees half buckle, "Not *here!* Beau?"

She swallows to keep herself from pleading, Please not in this Grecian glade where Stew and I — no, not this one, but the one like this one. She shakes her head, exhausted, confused. Beau is already striding away, all business. She watches him disappear when he steps into the tree line. He is gone.

She stands by the pool formed by mica-layered rocks. A last angle of afternoon sun rays through to create a colorful shimmer. Water cascades from stream into pool and out again much more slowly. She is mesmerized by this flow and exhausted by this day, but is most of all truly amazed at actually having made it up and over one of these Himalayas — a foothill, yes, but still a Himalaya. She surprises herself with a full body ripple of self-approval.

Gingerly sitting on a flat rock, she sinks aching feet into the pool. It feels only cool, not the high altitude cold she expected, which makes her want to sink her torso in the deep end. Looking around, she wonders if her captor will be gone long enough for her to do that.

While she considers this, it occurs to her that to be able to wonder this at all Beau must have been gone quite a while. Her eyes widen.

Cecily scrambles up, adjusting her dress and peering around the clearing's edges. No one. She takes fast, tiptoed steps to the place in the trees they first broke through, and she pauses, head tilted for any hint of Beau's return. Nothing. Wait! No, nothing. She cautiously enters the forest.

She moves as quietly as she can through the scrub and over logs and around boulders back toward the path, finding herself feeling lighter. Her heart pumps with excitement instead of rage and terror. She keeps pausing and listening, though she doesn't know if she could really tell Beau's noise from any other. Maybe she can run back up the trail quickly enough that she could hide and wait till he went by looking for her, and then she could follow him back to that plateau, and from there she could find Kathmandu on her own, and then she would go to Anna's, he wouldn't find her there, and they would call the ambassador, he knows Stewart is gone for the summer and said to call if she ran into any problems, and she has run into one. Then she could take a bath and sleep all day and all night and Anna would fix her a big dinner and several drinks, and after a while Cecily would tell her everything that happened and Anna would say, No! That couldn't be true!

A touch hysterical now that she thinks she has escaped, she laughs exultantly to see the end of this criminal and insulting predicament. It is then that she runs right into Beau's arms.

They close around her, cradling her as she freezes, stunned, then struggles, then begins to scream, tearing at his arms and hitting him, screaming and screaming. Beau tries to still her as he is scratched across the face. He keeps saying, "Cecil! Cecil!"

But she can't calm herself, and her cries reverberate through the trees. He lifts her off the ground, but her flailing legs get in some hard kicks, so he drops her back down where she doesn't have as much room. Beau sinks lower and lower while holding her pinioned. She grows less and less able to move as he forces her to her knees. He continues to say, "Cecil! Cecil! Shut up!"

She gives no immediate sign of hearing this. Her struggles lessen only because she is immobilized by this monster holding her so damn tight.

Cecily soon has no choice but to quiet down because her throat is raw. She leans against Beau's chest, barely able to stay upright. After a time, Cecily raises her head and pushes him away. Feeble as the movement is, he leans back and gives her room. There on her knees, fragile now, she finally focuses on her kidnapper. Her eyes are dulled and no longer glow with terror. Terror just consumed itself in the pure flames of panic.

She croaks, "What, exactly, do you want from me?"

He pulls himself away a little more. He considers her, then gestures, "Carry the wood."

She staggers as he pulls her to her feet. He gives her a load of firewood to carry back uphill to the clearing. Soon, Beau is skillfully coaxing a fire from damp kindling, while she recovers with her bruised feet again in the water.

Later, he looks up and sees Cecily across firelight. He watches her put one hand up to her forehead, rubbing it back and forth, back and forth. The fire flares momentarily and haloes her tousled hair. Suddenly she yawns, moving the hand down to her mouth.

"Hey. Cecil. Get up."

He pulls her to her feet, getting her moving again with a brusque tone and forceful hands. He propels her out of the shredded thongs and unbuckles her belt. Suddenly wide awake, she jerks back from him, putting two meters between them.

He stands with the belt in his hands, frowning.

"Listen! You! Calm down."

Striding back to the pack, Beau kneels and digs around till he comes up with a bag of dried food, from which he flings a thick strip of meat in his captive's direction. She doesn't appear to know what it is.

Beau unclenches his fists and returns to setting up camp. Scraping a place free of stones and twigs, he flings flat a ground cloth and an insulator, then flips a bag over that, shaking it out a few times and letting it float down. He strings up a small tarp for shelter, even though there has been a four-day hiatus in monsoon and no rain clouds are in sight.

Then he turns to Cecily, who still stands listlessly between the pool and the fire, chewing carefully and holding the piece of dried meat with both hands.

"Bedtime, Cecil."

Paralyzed by this information, the tiny bite of meat half chokes her. Beau strips down to boxers, which makes it worse. Oh, my god. Cecily's mouth hangs open as he walks right toward her.

"Come, Cecil."

His softened voice, softened face by the last glow of light in the clearing, immobilizes Cecily as he closes in. But when he reaches to take her shoulders, she spooks and strikes out wildly. The punch she throws Beau catches, pulling her close where he pulls off her ragged dress. Turning away, he drops it with his own clothes by the sleeping bag, and then he returns to smothering the fire while she backs away again to the edge of light.

When she finally looks up from trying to cover her three parts with two hands, the wispy underwear more suggestive than full nudity, she sees Beau crouched over the fire. His long shadows are eerie. Omens crawl across her skin. She looks away and bites her lower lip until she inadvertently reopens the cut there. She moans softly, swallows carefully.

"Come here, Cecil."

He stands, his body language serious. She hurriedly comes. She has learned now what will happen if she doesn't.

"Yes, yes, that's it. Come on."

He gives her a little push to the tarped area. She stands there awkward and shivering, but not from the cold. She is ordered to get in the bag. When she stays standing frozen still, Beau walks purposefully to her, causing her to cringe.

He takes her jade-protected wrist and pushes her, rather gently, down inside the bag. Slipping in beside her, he zips up the side, then adjusts the near empty pack as their pillow. Lying on his back, he arranges her in the crook of his arm, her damp hair on his shoulder and her face toward his chest.

He asks if she is ok. She squeaks incoherently, tense all the way to her toes. Beau says, "Good," and orders her to stay in that position all night.

She can almost hear him click over into sleep, with her lying there by him shivering for a long time before she stumbles into a more tortured form of slumber.

26

WHEN SHE OPENS HER EYES to morning, Cecily is immediately awash in clammy panic. She cautiously peers at an extreme close-up of Beau's stubbled chin. Turtling up, she realizes he's lying there eyes wide open to the sky; unnerved, she sinks back. Her eyes dart anxiously between chin and forest edge. She is alive, ok. But she really needs to pee.

"Uh, Beau?"

"Hhmmm."

"I, uh, need to, excuse me, get up. Soon."

Pulling her along, he sits up in the bag and unzips it, flopping back the top to let her out, exposing them both. She is stiff; it's hard for her to move as she draws her legs up and out of the bag, stands, finds her leather thongs, then stumbles off as fast as she can without actually running.

Using fresh leaves to dry herself, she shudders at the experience of defecating in the woods. She is almost positive someone watched. But when she steps out from the tree line, Beau is kneeling by the stream washing his face, and he's clearly been there the whole time. She hovers under the last tree wearing nothing but crumpled, used underwear, her leather thongs, her gold earrings and a jade bracelet. She considers cowering there forever but finally moves.

Her back remains to Beau as she picks up a limp, soiled dress. Sweat stains seem darker than last night, how could that be? She sniffs the dress. Her mouth puckers with dismay, and she reluctantly pulls it over her head and cinches the leather belt, then pushes her hair back from her forehead and holds it tight, tight, tight, struggling to get a deep breath.

She washes her face and neck and arms. Drying with the bandana, she realizes with fury that Beau is watching her intently. Then he nonchalantly turns back to packing his bag.

Breakfast is dried strips again, but this time Cecily is glad for it, she would welcome anything this morning, and she chews until her jaws ache. Water buffalo jerky, she thinks, and is this other stuff dried persimmon?

As she chews, she surveys the glade that doesn't look so Greek in daylight. Chewing, she watches Beau strip the clearing of all signs they spent time here. She chews and wonders why she isn't hatching an escape plan: it's not like her to be so planless.

Beau abruptly takes off across the clearing with the pack on his back, gesturing for her to follow. She spends the rest of the morning scampering to keep up. Since she isn't leading today, and since they aren't trudging up some unholy incline like most of yesterday, she has more opportunity to look around. For a time they stride on through the same forest. Smaller paths twist off to uphill or downhill obscurity. On one occasion they meet some girls collecting wood, and another time they step off the path to let a heavily laden group of locals plod by. Lord knows where they all live, she thinks.

She observes them all look quickly away from Beau, sensing a rogue male, yet each stares openly at her. Her inferior status is obvious and they speak among themselves at the sight of such a memsahib. Cecily can tell.

Why she isn't attempting to use these people as rescuers and protectors from Beau, Cecily can't explain. All she knows is it just isn't like her to act this way. It isn't.

When they halt for lunch at a village Beau calls Bonsbote, he sits in silence on one side of the dung-rubbed porch of the largest house in town. Inside, a woman fixes food for them. The cook snorts derisively when Beau accepts her price without bargaining. Cecily asks herself where he suddenly acquired this endless supply of rupees.

Sitting on the other side of the porch and trying to cover her legs, for they are causing a stir among the locals, she wipes her neck with the bandana. She has wet it with water from a nearby clay jar; she hopes no one will mind. She keeps trying to remember local rules about what is *juto* and what isn't so she won't ruin someone's day, although up to now she has effortlessly succeeded in providing the entertainment of the week. A lineup of villagers gathers around staring at her, squatting and whispering and giggling.

It wouldn't be so annoying if the audience were just children, but everyone in Bonsbote is here. She turns away, drawing her legs up and pulling her dress down as far as she can. She considers draping the bandana over her face.

Instead, she stares out over the heads of the villagers. They wear none of the fancy dress some tribes wear, none of the heavy jewelry which often amounts to small fortunes worn on women's necks and arms, pierced into ears and noses. In Kathmandu, some women wear all that plus those five-meter *saris,* but these women wear simpler, more sensible outfits. Cecily shakes her hair to ward off the flies while everyone points and comments.

It disconcerts her to sit here being snickered at, she who has always tried to be tasteful. Glancing down, she reassures herself that her legs are still covered. Stewart informed her when bathing in a river or relieving herself somewhere at the edge of public, if she exposes herself accidentally it is ok, no one will mind, it isn't as if they never see naked bottoms. After all, the children run naked till fairly old, and then their mothers put shirts on them before bottoms. It is, he lectured her, that in their poverty they have to make something precious, something to be savored privately, so they cover up their women. Stewart says even after marriage he's heard some husbands never see all of a wife's body at any one time.

Cecily can understand this. She needs both passion and love to feel ok about revealing her body to any man. Obviously, tons of women here in Nepal aren't in love with their husbands. Does that mean love is a leisure time phenomenon? She thinks maybe yes to that question.

They sit there out of the late morning sun waiting for *dhal bhaat*, with Beau on one side of the porch and Cecily on the other and neither speaking, just occasionally eyeing each other. She sighs. Such a quiet twelve weeks had stretched ahead of her on that last day of school. It had seemed a time to heal after Joel's visit and what he'd told her about Stewart. Shifting uneasily on the dung-stained porch, she still does not want that to be true.

Then this crazy Beau came along and decided to play with her, to play little games that have mushroomed into an endless mess. She feels all the wounds, all the aches up and down her body, all now enhanced by a night on the hard ground. Cecily projects murderous thoughts at her adversary, who appears to have forgotten she is there. He reminds her of a cat who forgets about the captured lizard until the lizard tries to move, the cat then reaching out a lazy paw and slapping off another limb.

So why did she let it go so far? Why didn't she confront this cowboy from Hell the first time he bothered her? She willingly gave him power over her libido and her life, and look where it's brought her.

She dwells morosely on her plight. Hungry and uncomfortable and already exhausted before noon, she finally gives up examining why she is here and resignedly sinks into the muck of this predicament. Here with Beau. With Beau here. After a couple of minutes of these spiraling thoughts she catches sight of some trekkers coming up the path to Bonsbote from the north, and another few seconds pass before she realizes what she's seeing.

Westerners! Oh god! Westerners, oh lord! Thank you, Saraswati! Bless you, Bhairav and Allah and Buddha, yes!

Has Beau noticed them? No, he's still staring out over a panorama of unusually cloud-free Annapurnas that are breathtaking from this point of view looking west and north, seldom seen clearly at this time of year. She swerves her eyes back to the trekkers.

What should she do? What, what, what! Just get up and run? Beau shifts a leg and she jumps, her heart racing. Yes, she has to run. They are coming close enough now, she can almost hear their voices. She swings her eyes over again: Beau appears still lost in contemplation of the mountains so she cautiously moves her legs off the porch, pauses, moves again.

Then, she leaps up and catapults through the crowd of squatting villagers. Waving her arms, she shouts out incoherently. Oh god! The relief of it! The trekkers are headed south, she can go with them back to Kathmandu. They will save her!

As she runs, she hears the unmistakable yell, "Cecil!" behind her and knows Beau is following fast. She runs harder toward salvation, waving, shouting, "Thank god! Thank god!"

She stumbles to a halt, clutching onto the man first in line and gasping for breath in the thin air. She hangs on as he reaches out to support her.

"Cecil!" Beau's voice is urgent, a toxic hiss. He is now close behind her. She holds on tighter, overwhelmingly grateful to the small band of trekkers. She is saved!

It is then, just before Beau reaches her and puts one hand around her waist and the other on her arm and says, "Get your hands off him," gentle-like in her ear — it is then she realizes the small group of Western men are all Japanese.

All bewildered, non-English-speaking Japanese in a little group, smiling politely at her like they don't want to show that they think she is retarded. She is slow to understand this, only becoming alarmed when they all bow to Beau. She struggles in his grip. "Let me go! Let me go!"

But he holds her tighter. He spits out something harsh in a language she's never heard before, but she can easily interpret his meaning.

"I'm rescued, you asshole!"

"Oh, yeah? You think so?"

Beau's eyes are sheened opaque with rage. Then, to Cecily's dismay, he turns back to the astonished trekkers, bows precisely, and speaks to them in fluent Japanese.

She freezes. She gapes at Beau, aghast. She knows perfectly well what his explanation is: that she is mad, delusional. That she is more than likely dangerous and he's taking her somewhere safe. She droops. Oh god, she is done for now.

The Japanese trekkers click their tongues in concern and observe her politely, apprehension mixed with pity, and oh so anxious not to become involved in her pathetic tragedy. Cecily wilts. She feels the blood leave her face, and, not for the first time since this misadventure began, a ghastly weakness insidiously, nauseatingly takes over her will.

With his arm around her and his head bent at an angle of grave concern, Beau turns her away from the Japanese trekkers. He half carries her back to the house, pushing through the crowd of highly entertained locals.

Up the steps and into the farm house they go, where the cook still bends over their lunch. Beau growls something and gestures to Cecily with a careless hand. When the woman points to the ladder in the corner leading up into a loft, Beau roughly pulls Cecily to it, then pushes her up the steps through an open trapdoor, shoving her hard so she tumbles into the low-ceilinged room.

She lies there, her cheek to a floor of packed clay over wood, while her tormentor follows her and then jerks the trapdoor closed. He crawls at her in the low attic with its small shuttered windows.

Beau flings himself on her, his one hand tight on her throat and his other in her hair. Cecily can't breath under his weight on the hard floor, but when she tries to move Beau holds her still, his lips pressing harder onto hers. It gets worse when Cecily feels she can't breathe; he is suddenly so enormous it's as if his mouth is covering her face, swallowing her whole.

When Beau moves his hand down her ribs to her hip then down her thigh, resting a moment before he begins gathering her dress up toward her waist, Cecily does struggle, but somehow he has a hundred arms; she'll never get away.

The folds of her dress come together easily. Beau moves one leg between hers. When his hand encounters her filmy panties, he hooks a finger inside and pulls them down to her knees, then uses his own knee to push them down farther, his foot pushing them off. His hand moves back up between her thighs and his fingers curl through hair fluffy and soft. Cecily tries once again to heave him off, but gets nothing but his hand rougher between her legs. He undoes his trousers, his movements much less precise now.

It is at this point Cecily finds one of her arms free. As Beau pushes aside his clothing and moves back up between her thighs, Cecily stares at her miraculously free hand. Beau breathes raggedly, blind now with need and rage, so Cecily grabs his nose and twists it as hard as she can. His small blink of pain makes her smile for the first time since Sunday morning.

Beau reaches up and removes her grip like it was nothing. It is her still-good left hand, which he viciously pinches hard till she cries out and her eyes tear. She now owns two bad wrists, a matched pair.

Holding her helpless, Beau thrusts up inside, pounding pounding, grinding around and around. Cecily closes her eyes, her heart wild in her chest. As he forces deeper inside and settles upon her, she hates herself for being so wet for him.

She hates herself even more when her legs curl up around his and hold on tight. She's his consort now and for the next thousand avatars, with no escape in sight.

27

RESTING IN MEAGER SHADE later that afternoon several hours northeast of Bonsbote, Cecily lies on the ground with her head in the lap of her abductor. The silence is dusty and sweaty and Cecily is a grimy mess, but after their extended lunch break in the loft, Cecily has kept up to Beau's pace with no complaints. Her reward is now a nap on the trail.

They have continued to meet few people on this path, which admittedly is an odd route to take if heading to Helambu. Beau says it is because people just don't hike as much during monsoon, and Cecily wonders, why then are we out here, but she knows better than to say it aloud. They have been lucky with the absence of rains.

But now with her head in Beau's lap, she watches clouds build up. The sun shines through steamier air, and with the rising humidity Cecily has never felt filthier in her life. She drowses in self-defense.

Beau says something about the view, she responds, and they actually drift into a civil conversation. For the first time they share personal information, as if presenting each other small gifts. Cecily learns Beau was a special operative in Vietnam, speaks Vietnamese, oh, and Russian, needed it, while he finds out Cecily was a part-time model in high school.

She discovers Beau was a special operative in Japan after Vietnam, speaks Japanese. And Korean. He learns that she simply won't eat organs of any kind, because of an unfortunate experience in her sophomore year.

They eye each other in mild alarm, reminded they are unrelated specimens of the same genus. Cecily finally inquires, "So why, exactly, are you here, in Nepal?"

His face goes blank. He finally says, "There's a meeting scheduled next month. Up north, on the Chinese border."

Her voice is a bit thinner now. "And why, exactly, will you be there?"

After considering her closely, Beau admits, "I speak Tibetan."

How many languages is that now, five? Eight? And he didn't go to college?

Mulling this over, Cecily grows drowsy again, drifts away to a more comfortable continent populated by more normal people. She stays there as long as possible, listening to Joni Mitchell and blending fresh raspberry smoothies.

"Cecil. Up."

He brushes a fly from her cheek. He pulls her to her feet and then up off the path.

"Beau!" She protests in vain. She stumbles up the steep hillside thinking, Uphill again? And thinking, Isn't this the wrong direction? When Beau stops, he pulls Cecily on up to him and wraps her in his arms. They kiss long and hard.

At first she finds it a turnoff to be necking behind a shrub on a steep mountainside, but Beau nuzzles her sweaty neck and pulls her body up against his, and she staggers at the heat radiating from her nethers, washing up and over her. Beau sits on a stump and buries his head in her belly. Cecily surges with lust. But when Beau begins pulling her dress up around her waist (and she doesn't have any panties anymore because they'd been left behind in Bonsbote), she tenses, paranoid of such exposure, no matter what her loins think.

Still, after Beau's mouth says hello to her bellybutton then drifts lower, and after he firmly places her on his lap and twists slowly up inside her, she leans over to bite his nose.

Cecily learns a great deal with his hands on her waist during this afternoon interlude on the steep north slope of Shivapuri. With her neck arched and her hands wound into Beau's hair, she gazes up at the cornflower sky filling with clouds, shadows now scudding across the ground. At the cooler air rustling up under her dress, she shudders, her *yoni* tensing tight around Beau's *lingam*. Light tinges to orange behind closed eyelids. They gasp, then slump together.

At last he pushes her to her feet. She sways. As they clamber and skid back down to the path, she feels warm liquid running down her thighs. Though this bothers her, she is reluctant to use her filthy dress as a towel.

When they reach the trail, Beau frowns as he assesses the sky. Mounting clouds now cast shadows over the next ridge north. He tells her they have to descend quickly to the river running between this ridge and that one, then they need to walk a few kilometers east down the wash, about two hours or so, to a place called Tala Marang, then turn north and head up into the Helambu region. If they don't stop at all, this will get them there by dusk. He points out that she will have to walk faster.

She does walk faster, often stumbling but managing to keep going. An hour down the switchback, Beau pauses and gazes out over the chasm they are winding into, a thousand more meters nearly straight down from this point to the river, and the ridge up the other side not nearly so high as this one but ragged and sharp and right across from them now. He turns to Cecily, saying, "We have to leave the trail. We've lost too much time."

She peers down off the path. It isn't quite straight down but near enough.

"What? Here?"

"Yes. It's not as bad as it looks." He watches her as he says this. Finally she nods, swallows, and gingerly follows him off the trail.

The shortcut does not go well. Cecily does not have practice doing this sort of thing, so she can not move down the side of the mountain with anything near his speed. Bounding from step to step with his knees bent like springs, Beau has to wait while she moves stiff-kneed down to him, holding on to every bush, her legs shaking. Beau grows more and more exasperated.

"Bend your knees, Cecil! Bend your knees!"demands her nemesis, and "Christ, Cecil! We've got to go faster!" and even "Shit! Look, it's going to rain! Come on!" he complains, for the next two hours.

Cecily struggles more with each step, so tired she is having trouble seeing clearly. Her knees hurt when she tries to bend them even a little, and they have begun to swell. Sweat pours down her dress in a spreading stain so that the fabric clings to her and sometimes twists between her legs.

She looks up at the sky darkening overhead, then at the mountainside around them. They've been dropping down through rice terraces, and a small village lies in the distance. Down one level to another to another. To get through these, they have to balance on little dirt dikes between the paddies, at least meter-deep water on each side and the mud deeper below that. As her shakiness increases, Cecily has a growing fear of falling in. So, with more effort she progresses even more slowly.

It is by this time very late afternoon, and they have traveled only half the descent. Beau's impatience with Cecily causes him to say things to her she does not have the energy to answer. With her balance disintegrating, she can't even look up.

Again she bites open the cut in her lower lip. It drips blood down her scraped chin and splatters her dress. She stands a few paddies up from Beau with her arms out to keep her balance. She tries to slow her pounding heart.

Looking down on him from her catwalk between rice paddies, Cecily conveys with a haughty stare her utter disgust for him. What the hell does he mean treating her like she is suddenly his personal albatross, when all she'd wanted was to go to a baby shower! The turd! Then she slips and falls into the rice paddy.

She squeaks and grabs for the side, but it crumbles in her fingers and she goes down on one knee. She flounders in the water and mud, panicking, then remembers she isn't speaking to Beau so isn't going to call for his help.

One of her thongs comes off when she pulls her foot from sucking mud. No! Shit! She knows she'll not find that stupid shoe until next dry season. Nevertheless, she reaches bravely down into the slimy water and gropes for it.

"I'd get out of there, if I were you."

She looks up at Beau standing above her. He is maddeningly clean.

"Well, I've lost my shoe."

"Yeah? I'll bet you've found lots of leeches."

For a moment this does not register. Leeches? Leeches! Oh, no. Oh no no. She stands, slowly, hardly daring to look. But her arm is clear of leeches and she laughs, breathless. Beau reaches out his hand, which she reluctantly takes, and he pulls her up onto the narrow path, drawing her along to a place below where they can stand side by side.

Cecily limps on her one bare foot. She feels she's survived everything now. Imagine, falling into a rice paddy. Imagine. However, if she were to look down at her legs she would not be so calm, but Beau has hold of one of her sore wrists pulling her to safety and she is concentrating too much on maintaining her balance to look down at her muddy legs.

"Now, Cecil, don't get all excited. Ok?"

She stares at him, then follows his glance downwards to her legs. They are dark with what she thinks, at first, is muck. Then, she sees part of this dark gook moving around, a little space of skin appearing here, disappearing. She grabs Beau. "Oh my god! Oh my god!"

"Calm down, goddammit! I've got to get the iodine."

"Jesus! Jesus!" she shrieks, holding on tight to him.

The leeches move up her legs searching for spots to clamp on and suck all her blood out. Cecily lets go of Beau and flings her arms wildly, almost knocking him over. He grabs her, yelling, "Stop it!"

He shakes her by the shoulders till she stops it. She stares up at him and whimpers, white-faced, "They're moving up my legs, Beau."

He strips his pack off, unzipping a side pocket and pulling out a small squeeze bottle, muttering, "I know, I know, just be still. Don't move. Here," he hands her the hem of her dress. She holds it up to her nose with her eyes closed, swaying.

Her legs crawl and tickle and she doesn't know what Beau is doing about it, but whatever it is, it is painless compared with her other injuries. Whatever it is, she can't watch.

"Please hurry! Oh god, please hurry!" She moans through clenched teeth, holding back the nausea she feels at the thought of these slimy bloodsuckers on her body. Beau seems to take forever killing them with the iodine. He curses, then says, "There's just so damned many of them."

Which is the wrong thing to say. Cecily feels quite faint. She tries to take her mind off what is going on by watching a cloudbank close down the sky. Off to the north flashes lightning, thunder rolling to them eleven seconds later. She knows this because she very precisely and carefully counts to one thousand and eleven. Beau pauses to squint up at the sky.

"Beau!"

"Ok, ok!"

He bends back to the leech removal. He says through clenched teeth, "We're going to get caught in this."

He states this as if she could have done something to prevent it. Cecily does not answer. He glances up at her glazed eyes, then back to the leeches. They are mostly gone from the front of her legs.

"Turn around."

When she complies, he picks up the muddy back of her dress and tells her to hold it up. She remembers she has no panties on but it makes little difference any more. Beau continues efficiently knocking off leeches with iodine tincture, while Cecily stands looking into the enormous ravine-like valley. The sun is gone already behind the mountain above them and everything just around them lies in shadow. Another hour of light, she thinks. She feels immensely weary now that she isn't moving, and they still have to reach the river, and then walk down it some enormous distance to reach shelter.

"How much farther is it?" she asks, holding the back of her dress up over her shoulders with her arms crossed in front. There is no response from her tour guide.

28

ANOTHER HOUR GONE. Shivapuri and the next foothill merge into a vee like a crotch, where mountains meet river. Just enough light is left to see this river not far below.

Cecily half runs with Beau pulling her along, barely ahead of falling down. Well, not always ahead, for she's already fallen twice, and the second time he dragged her a ways.

In the last hour this unfathomable man has changed from the aloof warrior who frightens yet excites her, to a sharp-tongued bully who sets her teeth on edge with his insinuating questions. Yes, she is aware it is her fault it took them so long to get this far. Yes, she knows it will soon be dark. Yes, she knows they'll probably be out all night because she can't bounce down trails like any basic hiker with even the mildest degree of training. Yes, she certainly knows all this by now.

Finally they stand on a well-worn path. Although she can't tell one trail from another, Beau feels positive this is the same one they left hours ago. Suddenly, a line of porters comes toward them from around the bend below.

Cecily steps aside to let the porters go by on their way uphill. The women gawk at her from under their burdens. She raises her chin. What do they know? What does she care?

The porters are beginning their steep ascent at dusk, all of them barefoot. They must know the trail really well, she thinks, to start uphill so late. Each carries a big wicker basket hanging from wide straps around the forehead and down over the shoulders. Cecily understands a porter's life expectancy is pretty short. Looks like hers might be too.

It is as the two groups are carefully passing on this narrow trail that lightning splits the slice of sky above them. Everyone stops and turns just in time to meet a roar of thunder rolling down the river wash. Close, very close. Cecily cringes, looks to Beau: his mouth is strangely white. She looks away.

Cautiously, she peers over the path edge, where there is a drop so vertical there is no shortcut available the last hundred meters of their descent, so they will have to follow the switchbacks from here on down. The view stuns her. A monsoon-widened wash spreads at least one hundred meters across and is littered with bleached boulders, really big ones. It seems all the white rocks in the world lie scattered down this river.

The Nepalis wisely take their time up the steep trail. One after another, porters appear around the bend below Beau and squeeze up past him, then squeeze up the trail past Cecily, and she backs against the uphill side as far as she can.

Suddenly, she feels something brush the back of her ankle. She jumps forward and cries out in the face of a heavily laden woman, who staggers in surprise and peers up at a strained angle because she has to keep bent forward to balance her load. Cecily wrenches herself straight. As the two try desperately to avoid each other on the precarious path, their hands accidentally touch. Lightning and thunder rip down the ravine.

Cecily shudders. She opens her eyes to observe the woman moving her hands strangely and spewing a rapid-fire tirade in some language she's never heard before. Resembling a hunchbacked gnome, the porter shows Cecily her palms in the universal signal for halt right there. It appears to Cecily in another glare of lightning that the woman's hands turn all the way around at her wrists. Cecily's skin tries to crawl off her frame. She flinches at the image of the porter shaking her fist at the next tidal wave of thunder.

At this point she takes a deep breath and steps forward to reassure the porter. Once again, she times her apology with a crack of lightning so close they inhale pure ozone as thunder beats at them. The porter sends up a prolonged complaint. Her agitated fellow porters continue to gather in a knot far up the path from such a foreign devil witch.

Cecily is completely unnerved. With legs like noodles, she tries again to get around the overloaded woman, but the porter crouches even lower and complains even louder. Cecily finally stands totally still, backed as far off the path as she can get. She attempts a sickly smile and holds her hands behind her.

After long seconds, the porter staggers forward a few steps. Cecily stands quiet except for her eyes. The porter glares at her while saying something hostile to the group still gathered way uphill.

Cecily is partly blocking the woman's way but cannot get any farther off this trail hugging Shivapuri's north face. The porter cautiously takes another step uphill. Cecily is a statue. Sweat builds across her forehead. The woman takes another step, and another. Sweat drips in Cecily's eyes.

That moment, something again rustles in the bush behind her. Rat, snake, whatever! Cecily jumps forward in a fit of panic. The porter wails and crouches pitifully, paralyzing Cecily once more in indecision. What the hell is wrong with this idiot?

Again there is a rustling in the brush, and she sees that it is — yes! It is a snake! Oh my god, a snake in the brush, now slithering toward her bare foot, and some crazy old coot isn't going to stand in her way.

Cecily leaps by, trying not to knock the woman over the cliff but not able to avoid touching her. She reaches Beau. He shakes her off and steps back in distaste, but she doesn't notice because she's looking back up the path to see if the porter finally exploded on the spot.

Not surprisingly, the overloaded woman is standing there perfectly ok now but still screeching at full volume. She abruptly stops, spits at Cecily. A gob lands right by Cecily's bare foot, splat. One heartbeat later, the downpour begins. A curtain of water hammers them all.

Cecily whirls to Beau, flinging water back into the rain. He is aghast, crying out, "My god! Look what you've done now!"

PART IV

A ROCK AND A HARD PLACE

July, 1978

Prometheus

"Then you will come to Insolence, a river
that well deserves its name: but cross it not —
it is no stream that you can easily ford..."

29

TWO HOURS LATER they aren't much closer to Tala Marang. Beau's small flashlight can't illuminate much detail through the rain. Shadows suggest spaces that aren't there, and holes that look shallow suddenly drop down at odd angles. Clothes plastered to their limbs hamper movement.

Every meter they complete is a minor miracle. At one point, the river swells across the wash, making them detour to shore where they claw their way through the mud and muck of the shallows. It is here that Cecily loses her other sandal. She has no choice but to continue barefoot, river swirling around her legs and rain running off her head. Rocks cut her feet, but her blood does not linger anywhere.

While Beau hesitates, futilely shining his torch in search of a better way to Tala Marang, Cecily leans on a waist-high boulder and pants till she can speak, then asks if they can't just stop somewhere. Find a little shelter? Beau's face is not visible in the shadows, but he makes noises she can't quite hear that add up to "forget it." She doesn't pursue it because after their brief stop she seems to have found a bit of wind, and since her feet are almost numb now she can wade and climb from rock to rock better than before. Second wind. Dying nerves.

During the next hour, their fourth on the river, the rain lets up some and there is a lifting of clouds above eye level. She succeeds in getting Beau to stop once so she can pee. This she accomplishes by simply squatting till he comes back to find her. Hoping he will let her rest, she shouts over the din, "Can we stop? Beau? I need to stop awhile. Beau? Can't we stop for even five minutes?"

No response. She looks around from her perch. The view as far as she can see is dark, dark, dark in all directions. She and her silent comrade balance on separate boulders, the spating river centimeters below. Wiping her face with the sodden hem of her dress, she inquires loudly, "Do you even know how far it is?"

Even with the river in her ears, she thinks she hears Beau gnash his teeth. He finally mumbles something.

"What?"

He speaks louder, but is still indistinct. She shakes her hair back and calls, "It's the river. I can't hear you."

He turns on her and glares through the gloom. She shrinks back while he grinds out, "I said, the last time I was here it wasn't like this."

She already knew that. They stay silent, staring off in different directions from their own rocks, separated by night and swirling water. She ventures, "Was that during dry season, Beau?"

She can sense his scowl scalding her; it perks her right up. Cecily rests her chin on her knees and stares at nothing.

30

THEY GO ON. Among the clusters of boulders and mud are occasional lengths of pale sand that stick painfully to her raw feet. She loses all track of time, partly because the sun had set behind one of the looming ridges much earlier than she is used to. They rest again. When she asks Beau what time it is, he peers at his luminous dial and replies, "Eleven-thirty," through clenched teeth. She is even more depressed: Eleven-thirty? This is by far the longest day of her life, and it doesn't appear near over.

A distant flash of lightning illuminates Beau on his rock. Cecily is taken aback. She's never seen a man look so defeated. She works up the tiniest twinge of pity for him because his bold gesture has become a disaster. But he was very stupid, not connecting river and monsoon. That is more than dumb, she thinks.

She feels generous to be pitying Beau, but pity might be all she has enough of to share. Well, she still has her dress. Anything else? The jade bangle and her gold hoops, she touches them with cold fingers. Nothing else, not even her virtue.

She squats with her face in her hands, elbows on her knees. They sit so long that Beau's silence penetrates her fatigue.

She looks up. A marginally paler sky limns the silent man's profile. His nose juts out. God! Beau's nose. Cecily feels herself so awash with this man, she almost rocks backwards off her rock. She certainly has every reason to hate him, but despising Beau takes him deep inside her heart.

Good lord, what has happened to her mind! Waterlogged? She can't still hold a passion for this imbecile? She cringes at the thought. She certainly isn't happy being damaged like this, so what is it about him that still holds her? She sighs: it's a symptom of how warped she's grown since monsoon began.

Her mind spins from place to place, syncopating with the river's rhythm. Water slides by, gravel growls and rattles. Cecily's head is bobbing along, only stopping when she feels dizzy for a moment, sort of confused. Lightheaded. What's wrong with her now? She lifts her chin and glares at Beau on his rock so close to hers. The bloody bastard. Dizziness washes over her again, and she holds her head to make it all stay still.

"Beau? Let's just stay here." Her voice is reedy with exhaustion. She wets her lips with her tongue and she is taken aback by their advanced state of cracking.

"Could we perhaps stop here?"

Still no response, but he is staring at her. She shivers with cold, asking, "Could we perhaps just share a boulder?"

Damn him, why doesn't he say something.

"Could you perhaps answer me?"

Nothing. The slimy gonad. She turns away from him, hunching toward another part of the ravine they are so irrevocably in.

She can't believe him. Here he's brought her, scared her to death and hurt her into cooperating with his every whim, and now? Now, after all she has gone through without complaining, except for screaming a little with the leeches — ok, and kicking him, and twisting his nose a bit — but after everything else now he won't throw a word in her direction. The loose-bowelled turd.

That's all right, she won't let him get to her, he will not madden her into another fit. That is probably the next step in his plan — his plan? His plan? Of course! How foolish she is to have been thinking of all this as simply a Cossack raider act. It is much more complicated, isn't it. Isn't it?

Cecily is unaware she is beginning to wander away from her rational self. Exhaustion and hunger have finally affected her reasoning. She thinks, Someone must have paid him to do this to me. Stewart? No no no no, not Stewart, she doesn't want it to be Stewart. Who, then? She considers people she knows, and comes up blank.

After all, who could be in Nepal two days and forget about monsoon? Especially during monsoon. Who? No one. Absolutely no one could be that unobservant.

So, it has to be Beau's own idea after all. His big joke on her for some reason, and the idiot got carried away. Now that she thinks about it, he must have been hanging around planning it since dry season. In the doctor's office that day, looking so damned healthy she'd even thought that he looked too healthy to be visiting a doctor. And in the bank with Sidney Morgenstern? He must have been following her the whole time! My god! My god. But why?

She looks over at Beau through narrowed eyes, coming back a bit toward reality. Could he have maliciously, pointedly planned this by himself? All of it? Then stalked her for months? She considers. No. She doesn't think so. Not Beau. No, Beau clearly thought up this caveman gesture in the heat of the moment after their argument in the bazaar.

Well, these things always come to an end, don't they, and she is ending this farce right now. She stands to speak, then goes all lightheaded, having to stay quite, quite still for a moment before squeaking, "Hey! You!"

He doesn't move.

"Beau! Look at me!" There is a shrill note to her voice that she can't seem to control.

He turns and peers at Cecily. Shadows make his eye sockets cadaver-dark. She gestures, flinging her arms, and barely holds her balance on the boulder.

"Did you hear me?" She tries to sound threatening. Beau hikes up one shoulder and turns his nose away. This, at least, gives her confidence he is listening and obviously wishes she would shut up. Fat chance. If Beau is listening, she's taking this opportunity to set the record straight.

"Well. Listen here, Beau. I'm not going to repeat myself." A slight twang from her very safe heart of America childhood creeps in. "You make me sick, Beau. All you can do is sit there turning your frigging nose up in the air. You! Hey, I'm talking to you!"

Beau sits turned away with his nose raised to the sky.

"You turn and look at me! You shit-bellied liver, you — Yeah, you, you're the one!"

She leans forward and shakes her finger at him. He has now turned around and is watching her.

"I think you sitting there like that is the most total complete turd-like act in the whole entire world, ever! I mean, I think you can't think. I mean, monsoon, Beau! Monsoon? Rain? Rivers? Come on!"

Beau clenches his fists. At least Cecily hopes he is.

"I take it I should have worn hiking boots to my friend's baby shower? Hey, I'm sorry about that. Slowed you down a bit, huh?"

Beau quivers, his arms stiff down his sides.

"You think like a castrated water buffalo, Beau, I can't believe you. I can't believe this," She waves. "You didn't even bring a tent."

Beau points a finger at her. "Listen here, Miss Sweet Ass."

"Hey! Go suck dog shit, Beau! You know what, you know what?"

Beau, closes his jaws on something he is going to say, his face as bleached as the boulders.

"You know what?" she repeats it once more for full effect, then, "I've met freaks in the bazaar who are more together than you."

She draws a deep, sweet breath, continuing, "I've seen addicts there who can tell when they need an umbrella even if they don't remember their own names. And you?"

She holds up her arm in righteous anger. She feels like Carrie Nation. Beau could easily shove Cecily Havenshack off that rock, but how can he argue with Carrie Nation? She chuckles scathingly. He shrugs and turns away. This infuriates her.

"You know what else I don't like about you, Beau?" She screeches this one across the river. "You have no," her voice goes shrill, "absolutely no sense of humor!"

At this, he suddenly becomes still.

"You couldn't tell a joke to save your life!"

With that, she turns her own nose up as far as she can without falling backward off her rock. She folds her arms across her chest. He looks at her, deflated.

The ravine suddenly illuminates. It thunders, rain sheeting across them, all beginning within seconds after Cecily finishes yelling.

Beau shines his flashlight over her. She winces in the beam, dim as it is. Her face goes sour. She can see he is blaming the cloudburst on her whining complaints: she's offended the sky. He points the flashlight beam up to his own face, giving vision to Cecily's river-bound nightmare.

"How do you manage these things, Cecil."

God, she hates that name.

31

THEY CONTINUE SQUATTING on their separate rocks. Beau leans forward with elbows on his knees, one hand hanging loose and one hand up to his face. In watery moonlight, Cecily regards his profile: it's still heroic. The bloody bastard just can't help it. She sighs and bounces her chin on the palm supporting it, pleased at how long they've stopped to rest.

She sighs again loudly. The rain lessened a while back and a sliver of moonlight swam over the ravine, but Beau has made no move to leave. We should be moving, she thinks. We'll lose the moon soon enough when it finishes with our little bit of sky, and then we'll be left once again stranded in the middle of the longest night ever recorded. Her flesh crawls on top of an ever-present shiver from river air. It grows quieter, as if the river is taking a break, too.

Beau hasn't seemed to notice the weak moonlight, and she won't point it out because she isn't speaking to him. She watches him, shakes herself and averts her gaze, then finds her eyes sliding back toward him. She doesn't want to stare at him, really, but her rock sits slightly behind his rock and the panorama has no other riveting features. Boulders lie everywhere else. She chastises herself. She looks out into the night. But her eyes, of themselves, slowly rotate back to this infuriating man squatting over on his rock.

Actually, what really bothers her is that Beau has almost turned his back on her. Well? So what? Cecily sits in thought. She breaks the long silence.

"Beau? Why, exactly, did you do this to me?"

For a moment he says nothing, then he shakes himself and returns from far away with, "Huh?"

"I asked you why you did this," she repeats, forcing patience she doesn't feel.

His mind is obviously turning to her like a tugboat pulling a barge. Trying to haul in some plausible excuse, she surmises. Ok, what will it be? Because he wanted us to talk, like he first claimed? Bullshit. Because he wanted to hurt me? More likely.

He regards her seriously, then shrugs, "I don't really know."

He continues, "You were just so damn cute, spooking yourself every time we met." He pauses, then adds, "And you were just so clean."

Cecily, fascinated, echoes, "Clean?"

He thinks it over. "Well, yeah. Clean."

Beau elaborates, oblivious to her stunned expression, "So I decided to take you out of your enchanted palace and shake you up a bit, and at the time it seemed the perfect solution to our, uh, your, uh ... well, I was pretty fed up with you, and you know why."

Beau says the last part almost flirtatiously. She can't even respond. The man speaks a hundred languages and he can't think in any of them.

He continues almost to himself, "You were so tidy, so perfect. And shy, too, like a little duck I had once."

"A duck?"

"Yeah," he recalls, hunching into his memories, "a little duck."

She shakes her head to clear it, repeating, "A duck?"

"Yeah," he says, "but that was years ago. It's dead."

This isn't encouraging. She is out in these monstrous tooth-mother mountains with someone who can't account for his actions. He can't even make up a decent excuse.

The situation is inexcusable. If she ever makes it back she will never be the same. She may not even make it back if she comes to more closely resemble his little duck. Beau is obviously irrational and his actions are unforgivable, but even a weak excuse, plausible or not, would make up for a lot.

Rain slogs down yet again. Cecily finds that water running down her nose bothers her the most of everything. If she closes her eyes, her discomfort grows. So, even as fatigued as she is, she keeps her eyes open and roving, stopping, focusing, blinking and itching from exhaustion.

Another pain makes itself known: her knees have ached for a long time now, and if she doesn't stand up she will soon be crippled. The process of standing up is difficult.

Once there, she stretches, not too far. Odd, the night is growing warmer now. Stewart explained something about that once, what was it? She hastily veers away from an image of her husband. She's been with another man now. Even if it was more or less against her will, the thought is inexplicably exhilarating, so perhaps that is what's warming her. Certainly, thoughts of Stewart have held no heat for some time. She crooks her hands up under her armpits and slowly swings to each side. Ahhh. This feels good.

It's something about altitude, that's it. This river bed probably sits at the same altitude as Kathmandu Valley, even though they are a couple of ridges farther north into the main Himalayas. She does a modified back bend. Stars overhead remain invisible and clouds swallow the last of the moon.

And there was something Stewart said about cloud-covered nights being warmer, she forgets why. Something about keeping the heat contained. She yawns hugely with her arms up over her head.

Beau, a statue for the last half-hour, makes no sign he remembers she is with him. She wonders if he's asleep or thinking. Asleep would be insulting, and if he's thinking it would certainly be nice to know the topic upon which he's able to focus his minuscule reason.

Below her, water rushes past through the blackness, eddying upon her rock, moving rapidly, but thinly spread over this part of the river. A nearby cliff, black against black, rises straight up for hundreds of meters before it begins to lean away and continue still farther up and up. And up.

She tries to touch her toes. That feels good, very good, bending the other way for a while. After several of these bends, she almost topples forward, and has to catch her balance quickly before falling off head first. Embarrassed, she peeks quickly to see if Beau saw, but he's in his own world.

Her heart pounding from exertion, Cecily sets herself flat upon her rock. She gazes around from her seat, holding her neck straight with her palms lying upward upon her knees. She breathes deeply, exhales slowly.

Beau clears his throat and speaks. "Huh, Cecil."

She can vaguely see him in the gloom. Clouds are once again sinking down to their personal altitude at river level.

Beau hesitates, "I, uh, have a joke to tell you."

He is kidding, she thinks.

"I don't think you're right about me, about me not having a sense of humor," he pauses, "so I'm going to tell you a joke."

She doesn't dare move: A joke? He's joking. But no, he drops his hand from his nose and swivels still squatting toward her.

"This is an ethnic joke," he explains, "and you've got to answer, when I ask the question."

She nods, speechless. Beau takes a deep breath. "Ok. So, how many ethnic terrorists does it take to kidnap the ambassador's son?"

She just stares at him. He's actually planning to joke about kidnapping? Then she remembers she's supposed to say something. Hoping her incredulous silence has not ruined the moment, she answers from her rock, "I don't know, how many?"

Beau, rigid while waiting for her to ask, quickly says, "Twenty."

He swallows and continues, "One to kidnap the ambassador's son, and nineteen to write the ransom note." He swallows again, audibly.

From her perch Cecily stares slack-jawed. Not bad, not bad. Her brother used to make up jokes, too, and this is better. She even smiles at Beau in the darkness and says, "Yeah? I hadn't heard that one."

But Beau, just to make sure she got it, explains, "You can put in anyone you want, you see. French, Australian, like that."

Cecily chokingly replies, "Oh? I see." Doesn't he know a joke's not funny if it has to be explained?

Beau falls silent, so she strangles out, "That's pretty good, though, with just 'ethnic,' I mean I like it that way. You know, with just 'ethnic.'"

He nods, "Me, too."

He adds, "I think it's funnier that way."

She agrees, still amazed at his insensitivity. He doesn't seem to have made the connection between his joke and the situation he's dragged her into. He then swivels back to due north on his rock, and raises his hand once more to balance his nose.

There comes a gusty whooshing from a little farther up the ravine, and they crouch under another downpour on its way down river.

Beau turns to Cecily, but she leaps to her feet first and points at him, crowing, "Ha!"

32

SHE QUIVERS AGAINST a desperate need to sleep, maybe to go unconscious. She knows they will have to do something soon. They will have to find some kind of shelter as Cecily wants, or they will have to keep moving as Beau wants. One or the other, there is nothing else.

Beau suddenly shakes his wet head, clears his throat, and Cecily thinks, Uh oh.

"I think," he states, "I think we should go for more distance." She pretends not to hear.

"It will keep our minds off the rain."

She turns away from him as he continues, "Then we can rest when it stops."

Sure, she thinks, insult my intelligence again. Beau adds, "If we continue sitting here on these rocks, we'll still have as far to go when the sun comes up."

She sniffs. His persistence is dogged. "If we start now we'll be there before dawn."

She rolls her eyes.

"And then we can rest a while in Tala Marang, eat, like that."

He'll never stop, she knows this. He'll never stop till he wins or she's dead. It's all so clear. Cecily is suddenly furious.

"*Dhal bhaat. Tarkaari,* maybe. At least *dhal bhaat.*"

"Yummy!"

He is silenced by the rage expressed in that one word. Cecily inquires, "And?"

Beau swallows. "And then, uh, then we can start up a few villages toward Shermatang. Rest there for the afternoon."

She blinks, astounded. "Start up? Start up? A few villages?"

"Well, uh, yes."

She waits for him to explain his marvelous plan.

"We could make up for lost time, you see."

Silence.

"Cecil?"

Cecily feels no need to respond. Let Beau take his idiocy for as long a stroll as he wants, she isn't about to leave this rock if that's his wonderful plan. He really is a waste of space.

He shifts his weight on his rock, trying to sound reasonable. "Cecil, we need to keep going."

She ignores him with her back stiff.

"Listen, ok? We'll stop in Tala Marang and stay till afternoon. Till late afternoon."

She keeps her face set and her spine rigid.

Finally he spits out, "Ok! We'll stay the night in Tala Marang! But we head up tomorrow."

Cecily surprises even herself with the vehemence of her response. Maybe the constant drip-drip-drip on her head has something to do with this.

"I'm not going!"

"Cecil," Beau stands and bends toward her threateningly.

She grinds through her teeth, "I'm not!"

They glare at each other. She struggles up, standing so he won't tower over her.

"You're going!"

"I'm not! I'm not going anywhere else with you ever ever ever!" She shrieks, "You poor bastard, you can't even tell a fucking joke the right way! Why should I follow you anywhere!"

He hisses, "I'll leave you here!"

She leans forward, her eyes wild and her arms waving. "You'll leave me? You'll leave me! I can believe that, oh yes! Well, that's the best news I've —"

"You're going!" Beau leans forward and grabs one of her gesticulating arms. He jerks as hard as he can and then thrusts her away, and begins trudging to Tala Marang come Hell or high water. His back is turned when Cecily's voice is drowned in the splash she makes as she goes face forward into the water.

She breaks the little finger on her right hand as it bends backward under her weight. Then, as she goes down through the madly swirling river, she breaks her nose on a large rock lying just under the surface.

Cecily blacks out and breathes in two full lungs of water.

33

BEAU IS NOT AWARE OF what is happening until he realizes Cecily is not behind him. Staggering back, he stares, then quickly pulls up on an arm to lift her out of the water. This would have worked fine if she'd been conscious and able to help.

Unfortunately out cold, Cecily swings and twists in the current, then swirls so the back of her head clunks heavily against the very same rock that broke her nose. Fortunately out cold, she doesn't notice this.

Moving fast, Beau scoops her limp form out of the river. He grabs her around from behind and squeezes hard. Water spews. He repeats this twice more, hard, just to be sure she's emptied, then he lays her on his rock. She hangs over all the edges.

Panting now and peering around for a better place to put her, Beau spies a big boulder, flat-topped and about chest high. He hauls her up and somehow balances from rock to rock above the river. After lifting and rolling her onto the flat surface, he hoists himself up and kneels beside her.

Drawn in a thin line under his nose, Beau's mouth is as white as the boulders. He hesitates before touching Cecily's pulse. When he does, its flutter is reassuring. She is bloodied but alive.

Methodically, he tests each part of her body as he shifts her to a more natural position. The legs seem all right. He moves the joints. Pelvis ok, hips — he lingers at Cecily's hips before moving north. Ribs feel all right — no, here's a break, right side, third rib up, ouch. Ok. Shoulder normal, elbow bends, wrist, fingers — right little finger, broken. He reaches for his pack upon which to rest this hand, then he moves over to her left side.

All this so far is checked out in darkness. For his inspection of her head, Beau pulls out his torch. He admits that her continuing unconsciousness points to a head injury. Otherwise, she'd be moaning and retching all over the place from nearly drowning. Unfortunately, a head injury is what he can do the least for out here in the middle of nowhere in the middle of the night.

He hesitates another moment, then shines the weak beam at Cecily's face. He sucks in his breath: her nose is already swollen up into her forehead. Blood streams out her nostrils. Beau moves the light and gasps, "Holy mother of god!"

Taking care, he moves her head, searching for more wounds. He finds a badly swollen spot on the back of her skull, which he avoids touching in case of bone fragments. He is reassured to find no blood leaking from her ears or eyes.

Gently he turns her head to one side. He sits back on his heels and stares at her. It strikes him that she might have trouble breathing with that nose. What is he supposed to do for a broken nose with simultaneous skull fracture? Sit her up or lie her down? Seeking the gloomy heavens for an answer, he hunches his shoulders against an insistent rain and turns up his collar. Fat lot of good it does.

Long minutes pass there in the slogging rain before Cecily gasps and sputters, approaching a state of semi-consciousness. Beau crouches over her, relieved at this first sign of life because the longer she's out, the worse off she'll be. When she stirs again, he shines the torch in her open eyes. They remain dilated even in the sudden glare, then they roll up and she's out again. He switches off the torch, saying sharply, "Cecil!"

A small fluttering of her eyelids. Her face is ghastly pale, even against the color-leached river rocks. He leans closer and repeats, "Cecil!"

This time her eyes come wide open and she stares up at her rescuer. When she tries to speak, her face refuses to cooperate. Her injuries are already moving away from numb at a fast clip toward true agony. Beau orders, "Don't move, Cecil! You've gone and hurt yourself."

She swallows with difficulty, then croaks, "My face?"

He looks away, adjusting her arms and legs.

"Yes. I think it's broken. Your nose, I mean. And don't move your right hand, ok? You've got a broken finger there. And a broken rib, same side."

He keeps his eyes averted as he tugs down her dress, continuing, "You'll live, Cecil, just don't move around, ok? Just stay still."

Cecily tries not to panic. She struggles against a complete breakdown at facing the brutal reality of her life. Beau crouches there rubbing a hand up and down her cold, wet thigh.

Time passes. The rain does not cease. Cecily swims back from another dizzy darkness, angry to find consciousness so much worse than dizzy darkness. This time she also feels gravel prodding her backside and rain plopping heavily on her front side. Drenched, she shivers convulsively. She just might howl, but when she draws her face up to do so, the distress grows into something much worse. She tries to relax, but cannot regain that previous, less painful state. Then Beau starts to move her.

She moans. Her teeth chatter. She looks up at him as he begins lifting her and sliding something under her neck. Why elevate her head? Not good, not good! She gags in pain. That over, she feels momentarily struck by the volume of Beau's shallow breathing, then realizes it is her own breath that is so loud, so fast, so inadequate.

But with this slight elevation gravity comes to the aid of her damaged respiratory system and oxygen once again finds her bloodstream. Cecily grows calmer, lies limper. Beau sets about gently lifting each part of her body to brush rubble and rocks out from under her, but she's also lying in several pools of rainwater that he can do nothing about. When her right arm is lifted, the pain in her little finger feels far removed, far distant from her face and the back of her head, which has made itself known. She thinks it best to lie quite still with her hands down her sides. And after Beau has done what he can to make her comfortable, she passes out again.

She floats in and out of awareness, while Beau sits watching her. If she moans or stirs, he leans over and pats her till she quiets, then rocks back on his heels. He peers at his watch with the weakening torchlight: 3:30 a.m., two hours to go till dawn. He glances at Cecily lying fitfully asleep, then stares back up at the sky.

34

RAIN SPLASHING NEXT TO HER ears awakens Cecily. She feels a little clearer about events, but not any happier. It's so cold and wet that still being alive isn't that much consolation. When she shifts a bit to find a more comfortable position, pain takes away her breath. Even blinking back tears hurts.

Later, she looks down her torso past her feet into darkness. With this effort her eyes cross, and she has to fight to refocus them. She can see the twilight world she is part of ends at her toes. By slowly swiveling her eyes, she can see the right side of her platform about one meter away, but she can't manage to move her eyes far enough to see the left edge. She also cannot see Beau. Where is he? My god! However, after this moment of panic, moving her head needs a better reason than just locating the fool who got her into this state.

Cecily would like not to remember how this happened, but she recalls all too vividly falling forward into the river. She remembers water and the crack of that collision between rock and nose. She will remember that sound the rest of her life, brief as it's likely to be.

She shudders. This unforeseen movement brings on unbearable spasms of pain. She moans and tries to stutter out "H-h-," but that also hurts. Trying again, she finds whispering less painful. "Help?"

At once Beau crouches at her left side. "Cecil? Awake now?"

"Yes," she whispers.

"How you doing?"

Bloody fool! Idiot! She moans in frustration and even regrets that.

"Do you want me to move you? Your legs?" He reaches.

"No!" She cries in panic, then is paralyzed by agony.

He looks out to the far side of the wash, then back down at Cecily. He begins to say something, but closes his mouth and looks away again. Her pain is suspended by incredulity: Is Beau about to cry? She can't see so well.

Beau finally stammers, "Cecil, I, I have to leave you. For awhile, I mean."

Beau uneasily continues, "I have to go for help. Soon. So I can get back here before the sun hits you."

He looks knowingly upward and clears his throat. "You see that, don't you? Because otherwise I'd never leave you alone like this." She listens to him convincing himself. "But you're way up here on this rock, well over a meter above the river so you should be ok. From the river."

Still she does not respond. Beau hurries on. "See, if I go now, I can probably make it to Tala Marang in an hour, even less. Then I'll round up some people and get a litter, they must have one already because that's how they get out of here themselves when they're, uh, then just another hour back here to get you, and by that time it'll be early morning so we'll find you, easy."

He rushes on, doomed to disappoint Cecily. "Then we'll get you out of here to somewhere we can fix you up, splint up that finger, find something for your face. And the back of your head? Well, it's kinda bad. And then there's your rib. Well, we'll just have to rest a while like you wanted before starting for the Chinese road, and I promise you, Cecil! I'll be back here as soon as possible."

He hesitates yet again. "Can I do anything for you? I mean, before I leave? Because I have to go."

She stares at him through two black eyes that barely slit open. Beau nervously offers, "Would you like my shirt? To cover your legs?"

She whispers, "Yes."

He strips it off, leaving him in a wet undershirt plastered to his torso. He asks, "Anything else?" with some authority back in his voice.

Cecily feels the palpitations of his anxiety over leaving her. She holds him with her eyes while she thinks, her green eyes now dulled to mud. She whispers, "Yes."

He has to lean forward to hear her croaked whimper.

"Will you prop me up? Sit me up more?"

He looks at her, then around, and she can almost hear him say to himself, What does she think, that I brought a beach chair?

She croaks pitifully, "Please, I can't breathe. Beau?" Her voice trails off.

"Hey, hold on!"

She watches Beau as he crouches there in laborious thought. He brightens, steps to the edge of the platform saying, "Got an idea." He disappears.

Tears seep out of Cecily's eyes and roll unheeded down her temples and over her ears. She hears a splash breaking the continuous rushing of the river, then several splashes in a row, then a medium-sized rock clatters onto the far left of her platform. More splashing, another clatter, this continuing till Beau has maybe twelve rocks up on the edge there. She hears a whoosh as he pulls himself back up and squats, breathing raggedly. On his knees, he shifts the rocks closer to her head and begins to pile them in the fashion of a backrest as best he can in the gloom. It takes quite a while.

He leans back over Cecily and tells her he has to move her some. If she can just relax a little, because it might hurt. First, he helps her sit up. It is all she can do to keep her neck straight so her head doesn't fall off. Each centimeter of movement sends spasms out through her eye sockets. She stays valiantly conscious as Beau slowly lowers her and tries to adjust her limbs.

"Are you ok? Cecil?"

She cannot answer.

"Cecil? Can I change it somehow? Make you more comfortable?"

Her eyes are shut tight.

"Can you breathe any better? Cecil?"

She hears him so close. She hears crystal-clear the water swirling around, gravel crunching under its force.

Her left hand lies on something odd-shaped and hard. When she moves this with her eyes still shut, she discovers the lump is something inside her pocket, and she absentmindedly reaches into the folds of her dress until she finds it: the penknife.

Her penknife? Still here? Good. She can slash her wrists if he doesn't come back. Wait! Wait. Hmm.

And she whispers, "Higher. Can you raise me higher?"

He bends closer to understand her, then leans back again. His voice registers poorly disguised dismay. "Higher?"

Cecily whispers, "Please," so hopelessly that Beau has no choice.

She hears him drop off the edge of her rock, then the splashing and clatter as he begins piling up more stones. The task takes longer this time because he is near exhaustion. After he pulls himself back up he crouches by the new pile of rocks, wheezing this time. Then he drags each rock over to her side.

Sitting up is not as painful so long as she remains completely stiff and fiercely concentrates while Beau reshapes her backrest. When she sways, he lies her over to one side, still bent at an angle. She is briefly terrified he'll leave her this way. It takes him several minutes to fit all the stones together again and get her set up at a better angle for her shattered sinuses.

Pleased with her new sitting position, she feels much better suddenly. Beau stands up brusquely. Looking at the lifting sky, he announces, "I must go."

Cecily croaks something. He can't understand her, so he reluctantly squats again. Still, he can't quite make out what she's saying, so he leans closer. Cecily's eyes are almost closed as she whispers something. Frustrated, Beau puts an arm on either side of her and leans his face close.

"Cecil? You all right?"

It is then that she makes an almost languid motion, as if putting her hand up to his shoulder. Instead, she comes down fast and hard with the three-centimeter blade of the penknife right into Beau's forearm, just below his elbow.

She pulls the blade down, tearing as jagged a cut and as long a one as she can manage. She even thinks about which side of the knife will fold up and cleverly holds it the strong way.

Beau falls away with a howl, pulling the knife with him and clutching his arm. He lies for a moment motionless on the rock, then pulls the knife out. Panting, he huddles over his arm for a few seconds before crawling back to her with the knife in his death grip. Blood seeps from his right arm and splashes onto the rock as he comes at her throat. She can tell he wants to stick the knife in her and twist it good.

She whispers, "Ha ha, Beau."

She decides that whatever happens, whatever he does to her now, she won't let him know it hurts. She'll simply pass out, and that won't take much effort at all. But at least she struck back a blow to defend her honour and to begin her revenge. Yes, this was the launching of her revenge campaign, and Cecily knows she would feel prouder of herself if only everything didn't hurt so much.

Beau's glare grows more fierce, holds, burns, then vanishes, poof, leaving a strange expression on his face. Uneasily she watches his eyes alter.

"Cecil."

She doesn't like this. What is he thinking?

"I get your point."

A pause, then she rashly caws, "Ha!" Her face feels like it splits in half, her amusement ending in a raspy sob and extended moan. Beau smiles with genuine satisfaction at the success of his joke.

He announces he still has to go, now more than ever. He looks back while gingerly crouching on the edge of Cecily's rock. He smiles at her with something close to affection, and she attempts to return it from her half-sitting position atop a boulder in a white rock wash somewhere north of Shivapuri. Her only hope of rescue disappears with a splash over the side.

Cecily's view by now has crept out quite a ways under the changing of night to day. She gazes over scenery she expects will become very familiar.

A small noise draws her attention back to where Beau disappeared, and she catches his hand sliding out of sight after depositing her penknife there on the very edge of the rock. It is just out of her reach.

Just in case, Beau? Just in case you don't make it back?

35

TIME HAS PASSED. She knows this. She can tell. She lies rigid as the pain of her face and a walloping throb at the back of her head merge and diverge, merge and diverge, each time with a centimeter less space between. Soon the pain will fit tight like a swim cap and she doesn't know if she'll be able to survive it. In her lap, her left hand clenches so white it glows blue.

The rain has abated and daylight sharpens her. She is by now impressed with the amount of discomfort she has survived. This helps her feel not completely hopeless. If she breathes shallowly so her rib doesn't grate, and if she doesn't move her right hand around at all, why, it is actually interesting to look out and watch the sun arrive at her part of the Himalayas.

Beau has placed her with her back to the near bank so her view takes in a mountain just across the ravine and all the water and rocks in between. Above, pink clouds obscure her part of sky, then turn to gold and white with morning light. She watches one particular fleecy cumulus play bumper sky with other cumuli. She tries mentally steering it left. Yes! She tips it right against the wind and tacks north, floats it up, and then loses it behind a cloud now hanging big and sullen just over her head.

The knife lies where Beau put it a thousand hours ago. Cecily thinks idly that if she had it she could at least clean her nails. Well, perhaps not. Anyway, if she moves too much her head will crack open and her brain will fall out and land with a plop on this flat wet rock.

At least another hundred hours pass. Finally bored enough to attempt one small move, she cautiously raises her right arm, lifting her broken little finger to eye level, careful not to move her head even the teeniest tiniest bit. She is annoyed at the listless obedience of her hand, but closer, closer, ouch! Finally, scrutinizing her little finger, she observes it is jammed the wrong way out from breaking her fall into shallow water.

While inspecting her finger, she glances at, then comes back to marvel at one of the very first injuries she acquired from Beau: deep blue bruises around her wrist. She'd forgotten about them, and those on the other wrist too. She holds her arm higher to beam sunlight on the bruises still cobalt under the jade bracelet.

She decides this arm looks too thin to be hers, and then realizes all her bones seem to be jutting out. Suddenly she is starving. Starving! And thirsty! Thirsty and hungry! She clenches her thin hand without thinking and is punished by her broken pinkie.

Birds vociferously visit her part of the river. She can't remember if she heard a bird song at dawn, but who knows and who cares. Trying to stay coherent, she grimly watches for these birds, and when they do appear she tries very hard to identify them. This becomes important because she is so sleepy, and she knows falling asleep with head injuries is not a wise thing to do. She must stay awake. Daring to move her head and sincerely regretting it, she settles deeper into the morning.

In the next hour, Cecily identifies a half dozen different birds. Of these, she sees either several individuals, or the same one again and again. She most enjoys the antics of a common plumbeous redstart, with its spreading rufous tail and dark bluish body, because it so characteristically flits around the rushing water and perches upon boulders near hers. She says all this aloud to herself to stay awake.

There is not a great deal else to do. Since the morning continues cool, her feathered friends hop about happily. When the sun becomes too bright, too warm down in this white rock ravine, they will all fly away.

Cecily looks down at her sorry body. It lies all lumpy and sodden, boney, limply arranged. She feels like a paraplegic must feel, though she thinks they are mercifully free of pain. To her current regret she is not free of pain, and it looks like a stretch of time before she will be. Pain is her mantra. Pain's clarion is her symphony. Discomfort percusses and flutters. She jerks her attention away from this cacophony just in time.

Perhaps she can identify yet another bird. Yes, another bird. She stares feverishly at the scene spreading out in a maze below her toes. Wait. Is that a wagtail? Oh rot! It flies so, it flies away away so.

More time, much more time passes. A million hours, at least, before Cecily hears human shouts coming up the ravine from down river. Instinctively, she turns to the voices. This movement rolls her off her backrest and onto the flat rock that has become her universe.

Oh god. Trothed to pain. Not only has she fallen over, she has fallen over on her right side and landed on her broken rib and her hand with the broken pinkie is lying in a rain puddle after whacking against rock.

Cecily cries out wretchedly. Voices call back. She wails out her agony, and the search party calls back in a refrain of her pain. They are the chorus from hell.

But she can't let them find her like this! She has to be sitting up! She struggles, levering herself up somehow through sheer force of will and a sort of half push-up. In the struggle her head implodes and her other injuries inform her of the end of life as she knows it, but she endures all this excruciation till she sits again.

The humans sound closer. Sweat trickles down Cecily's thin grimy neck as she struggles valiantly to stay upright.

36

IT IS SEVERAL ETERNITIES later that Cecily lies drifting in and out of consciousness on the floor of a hut behind the Pomp and Joy Hotel in Tala Marang. At times she knows where she is, but at others she is still back on the river.

When the porters carried her around that last river bend, she saw that the top floor of the Pomp and Joy had no outside walls and stood completely open to the view. She expected they would put her up there. As she was carried under the eave of the hotel, Cecily believed she would lie up there looking down the river canyon because, by now, that's what she does best.

Instead, she is lying on the floor of this hut. She can't believe she's been through everything to end up stored like a sack of rice behind the kitchen. At this thought, she returns to a semi-conscious hover.

During the rescue trip down river, Cecily kept drifting off. What anchored her briefly was realizing that one of her saviors was a Peace Corps Volunteer who just happened to be staying at Tala Marang. He had bandaged Beau's arm properly and organized a stretcher and then rounded up the porters before leading the rescue attempt. And, he was someone she knew from Kathmandu.

When the search party clambered close to her rock, she recognized him from afternoons spent at Phora Dhurbar pool where he swam all the time; she had seen him a lot. He had even tried to pick her up once, at least she thought so at the time. Anyhow, he knew her!

Cecily wanted to die on the spot. Moving jerkily, perhaps hoping somehow for a miracle machine of escape, she instead just toppled over again, only to the left side this time. At least she was facing up river and away from them. If only she could have slithered right over the edge and into the water and drowned for real, that would have been more entertaining.

But they were all suddenly there upon her rock and leaning over her, a bunch of concerned faces floating like tethered balloons, so she must have blacked out for a bit. She first focused on Beau, his arm bandaged. Then that other face swam into view, and she cringed down into the rock, whimpering. They assumed her delirious. Beau clumsily tried to comfort her, which did not work at all.

They propped her up again. Beau and the PCV squatted beside her, discussing the best way to get her off the river. She could see the PCV drawing with his finger on the rock. She could hear the PCV tell Beau, "Yeah, somehow after you left Pati Bhanjyang, you missed the trail to Tala Marang."

He moved his finger. "You must have gone due north. I don't know how you did it, man, but you two ended up coming *south* down the Malemchi Khola," he said, gesturing at the river. "You must have hit it somewhere north of Mahakal, and there's not much up there."

He pointed at Beau. "That's why you were so turned around this morning."

The PCV looked at Cecily in disbelief. "Sure would like to know how you did it."

The porters smoked *bidis*, one of them laughing at another's comment. The PCV checked Cecily's pulse and adjusted her new emergency blanket. She realized then that the PCV did not recognize her. He had no clue she was anyone he knew. She decided to feel relieved about this, for if somehow she did survive this private apocalypse, she certainly did not want anyone to know about it.

But now, after lying here on the Pomp and Joy's unforgiving floor, she wonders how bad she must look for him not to have recognized her, especially after he spent the whole dry season staring at her across Phora Dhurbar pool. She raises her left hand to touch her face, but can't get through a wall of heat radiating from her injuries.

Four porters carried her over the rough landscape. It was when they tied her to the stretcher that she finally left her body. As the porters maneuvered through all the rocks, the actual real Cecily floated down river above her earthly avatar. Pieces of her old life floated along with her like really light luggage.

And now inside the hut with the morning advancing to noon, her thoughts turn gloomy. She considers the few sins she's committed in this life. Were they enough to earn this? Cecily contemplates her broken body. Even in the clarity that comes with an out-of-body experience, she cannot explain this ruinous debacle.

Had she somehow built up a load of black marks on some

unknown chart? All she remembers are some minor deceptions. Maybe she had played mean little games as an adolescent, told a few white lies along the way, perhaps even an occasional black lie, but certainly no heinous crimes and none of the greater sins. So, no. All of her transgressions multiplied twice don't add up to this reality.

Could she somehow have offended a more local god? Could it be one of Nature's bad-tempered jokes on Cecily Havenshack for always being so fastidious, so fashionable, so nitpicking scrubbed all the time with special soaps, and wearing clothes only once before making the *dhobi* soak them in imported, scented powders?

Well, if Nature found any of this offensive, then that Mother just paid her back royally, because out there on the river she finally hit rock bottom: she peed in her filthy dress.

If the rescue party noticed it when they moved her onto the stretcher, they said nothing. Because she was soggy all over? She clung to this explanation.

After an indeterminate period of time, Cecily reluctantly reinhabits her body and finds herself back in the pokey little hut. They had put down a few dusty old rugs for her to lie on, which is bad enough, but the straw about to break her back is she might have to poop in her dress.

Does she really, truly deserve this?

"Beau?" she croaks. No one answers.

"Beau?" A little louder, not much, and still no one.

When she calls out a third time, desperately forcing herself to overcome the pain of speaking, a small girl silhouettes in the doorway. Cecily pants shallowly through her mouth, whispering, "Beau. Bring Beau."

She can remember none of her determinedly learned Nepali phrases. Funny, she thinks, there are so many things slipping away, leaving all these gaps. It is, of course, a result of fatigue. Nothing more drastic is wrong with my brain, she repeats with conviction.

That she forgot Stewart's name this morning while still out on the rock and had to dredge up several memories of him before her own husband's name came back to her. Well, hmm. She doesn't know exactly why she was just thinking about Stewart, but she still has to poop and soon.

She croaks, "Beau *sahib?*"

If the girl would only move into the room so Cecily could see her better. She feels a small shifting in her bowels, and makes a slight sideways movement to the left toward the exit.

"Beau!"

A million needles shoot up through her face and forehead, drawing hot threads of pain behind. She groans. The child in the doorway does not go anywhere.

Cecily lies quite still. She just won't move. She isn't going to let her bowels get the best of her — especially since she will have to lie in it. Most likely she picked up some parasite, maybe when they ate at that one village the day before. She will likely acquire some other parasite in this village, if anyone ever feeds her. Oh, Beau, please hurry! Shadows in the room tilt as the girl in the door frame scratches her neck.

But Beau does not come and the girl in the door does not go. Cecily's abdomen writhes. She holds her breath. Perhaps it is just gas? Most likely it isn't. With years of experience under her belt, she doesn't think she's being bothered by a bit of gas. Besides a broken nose, a broken finger, a broken rib and a likely concussion, added to an array of cuts, bruises and abrasions, she is very, very clear she has a big one waiting to soil her dress and possibly the entire world.

"Beau oww!"

Oh, Christ. Oh, Buddha. Oh, Shiva the Destroyer. Oh, Kali, oh Saraswati, oh Mother Teresa!

Sunlight suddenly beams inside her hut. Cecily glances up to find the girl gone.

It is this movement of her eyelids that does it. The rest of her body she continues holding perfectly still. Thus is Cecily abruptly separated from her noxious burden, and her legs splay apart as the mess pours down between them.

She sobs, then gasps in agony. She lies there within that shaft of light as it bounces off dust particles in the fouled air.

37

RACKING, HICCUPPING SOBS dam up her throat. An odor rises, filling the hut. Cecily instinctively draws her bottom away from that in which it lies, but this allows the mess to puddle out, so she forces herself to lie quite, quite still despite her instinct to move to Portugal immediately if not last week.

When a shadow appears in the door, she prays it is the child returning. At least Nepali children would understand such a thing, it happens to them lots. Sliding her eyes over to catch those of the child, instead she finds Beau. Beau's puzzled nose works the air. Lines run deep down between his eyes.

She rasps despondently, "I kept calling you."

"I was with that PCV arranging — shit!" His nose wrinkles.

Cecily whispers, "Like it? Duty free." Tears well up, but she knows now better than to sob. Too much movement is bad bad bad.

Beau moves in to stand a tiny bit nearer. He begins to squat but doesn't make it all the way down. Horror crosses his face as he rises like a shot.

Tugged by gravity, tears run down Cecily's temples and puddle in her ears. Standing back in the doorway, Beau stares at her and holds his bandaged arm to his chest.

She's pleading now, "Beau? Please, can you, someone, please!"

Beau nods and disappears. She meant to call him back to tell him something important, but an unwise movement causes her to forget what it was. She strays across a vast landscape of discomfort.

Again shadow replaces light in the doorway. She can make out two silhouettes, one behind the other. When they move farther inside, she realizes the PCV who saved her has come back with Beau. Oh god, didn't he leave already!

The PCV squats near her, much nearer than Beau. He studies her with compassion and she thinks his eyes are beautiful without swim goggles. He moves his hand to her forehead, her ear, then to her wrist, saying, "Pretty hot, got a fever. Probably a parasite. Dehydration, exhaustion."

He keeps watching her, his expression puzzled. The PCV tells Beau to go get the hotel manager, tell her to come right over. Beau speeds away.

She tries calming her heart now pumping blood to her face. The last thing she needs more of in her head is blood, but it's such an effort and she feels so tired.

Soon there arrive more people than she thinks the hut should hold: Beau, the Pomp and Joy manager, the PCV and two local women, herself amidst them flat on the floor. The PCV converses with the three women in a form of Sherpa, while these women look upon Cecily with great interest. One bends and lifts her dress and peers underneath. Turning her head in pure shame, unmindful of any punishing pain, she catches Beau's putrid expression — then he gags at her smell.

Great. Just great. She hates him. Tears continue, her very own monsoon.

"Hey, hey, don't worry, ma'am! You'll make it."

Age abruptly falls upon her like dry leaves on a muddy path. Ma'am? Did he call her ma'am? The young and completely perfect PCV leans over and brushes wet curls off her forehead. It reminds her that men used to treat her like this, all consideration and tenderness. Before Beau. Before Stewart.

"These women here, I know them. These two are going to clean you up, ma'am, wash you all over and get you some clean clothes." He pats her, "You'll see, you'll feel a lot better."

He stands, "Just relax, ok? They're going to have to move you a bit, nothing unnecessary. You're going to handle it fine."

He is kind. Tears well into her hollowed-out response to his kindness. She has never known someone so kind.

The Pomp and Joy manager exits after a low-voiced conversation with the PCV. Turning to Beau, the PCV inquires coldly, "Coming?" Beau willingly leaves Cecily in the hands of the two women.

First, they sit her up, conversing with each other as they undo her dress which they push down past her waist to her bottom. They slowly lie her back down and place a soft cushion for her head. She appreciates the slight elevation, it lets her breath easier. She's starting to love these Tala Marangis.

One woman hammocks her bottom up, while the other pulls the tattered dress off over her hips, and they use it to scoop up the mess on the floor. It has been spreading underneath her for a lifetime. She quite happily salutes the demise of her pale peach sundress.

When the two women have the area cleaned to their satisfaction, one manipulates Cecily's limbs, while the other cleans her body with a wet cloth and a brass bowl of clean water. More blankets are spread under her. One of the two gathers up all the soiled cloth and steps out of the hut.

The one remaining lights incense, which works immediately on the atmosphere in the hut. Sitting cross-legged beside her on a newly cleaned floor, this woman begins to knead Cecily's legs, massaging her feet, stretching her calves. Cecily rocks softly.

The other returns with a bundle of clean cloth and more water in a brass urn heavy on her hip. Cecily lies completely limp to their ministrations. They can do with her whatever they want. What they do is wash her thoroughly, even her hair, and dry her with a rough cloth so her skin prickles. One of the two tucks Cecily's knees under her chin and sprinkles sweet-smelling powder all over her shiny clean bottom. She gurgles and chirps.

She barely remains awake while being dressed in a black robe, soft and warm on her now clean body. She barely notices the bitterly brewed tea they raise her up to swallow. By the time its painkilling herbs take effect, Cecily has dropped too deeply into slumber to enjoy it.

38

FOR THE NEXT TWENTY-FOUR HOURS, she drinks a lot of this bitter tea. Because of its euphoric effect, she loves everyone, even Beau, for pouring it down. They prop her up again, and she sits with toes to the door, looking out at a lovely back wall of the Pomp and Joy. A beatific smile lingers despite all the discoloration and swelling and blood seeping out her nose.

Onlookers come and go, often blocking her small view. She is aware even through her stupor that they have come to goggle at the injured memsahib who pooped in her dress. For the first time in her life, Cecily is the freak in the crowd. In the bazaar, people would throw money to make her go away.

Although she cares less than ever for Beau's company, that he's staying away bothers her. Makes her restless. When he finally does show up, he spends the whole visit not looking at her. He shifts uneasily while he squats between Cecily and the door. He explains to her in a monosyllabic spurt that the four porters are demanding double pay because of it being monsoon.

Then, "So, uh, can you guarantee them something?"

Beau has to repeat this twice before the meaning of his question penetrates her stupor: Does she have money? Of course she has money, Beau, she always has money. Does he want some? Didn't she already give him some? Again he explains about the porters.

"Oh?" Cecily repeats.

She agrees to give them all great fortunes if they get her back to her palace. He informs her he probably can bargain down, but she doesn't really care about getting a better deal.

At last he departs, her jade bangle clutched in his hand. She immediately falls asleep and poops in her clean clothes.

After another cleaning and swaddling, feeding and burping, the party readies to leave. She stands weaving, hanging between Beau and the PCV as they promise Cecily's money to half the Helambu region upon reaching Kathmandu. The porters immediately raise their price.

Her head aches abominably, and her puffed-out face squints horribly. When Beau poured a huge dose of sticky, bitter glop down her throat earlier that morning, he claimed it would make things easier for her along the way. It would stop her, uh, up. But, it is also making her nauseated.

Beau and the PCV continue discussing payment, and everyone forgets for a moment Cecily hanging there among them until she pitches into a nosedive. Beau and the PCV abort this by jerking back on her elbows. She blacks out after vomiting on Beau's boot.

They carry her back up and inside the hut to lie again on the floor, and Beau and the PCV return to arguing finances with the four porters. Cecily moans: her shoulders have been badly wrenched.

She breast strokes back toward a soupy, blurry consciousness when the PCV returns and squats down, Beau crouching behind him. Hearing her groan as they approached the hut, the PCV now makes her swallow yet another dose of the magical plant sap. It has become her diet.

Beau leans forward saying, "They want more money, Cecil."

He glances over to the PCV, then clears his throat, adding, "They, uh, won't take you without more money." The PCV sadly agrees, so she parts with her 22-karat gold earrings. The PCV holds her up and forward as Beau clumsily removes them. One ear bleeds.

After they give the earrings to the head porter, with Beau's pledge of more pairs of *memsahib's* earrings when they reach Kathmandu, the group once again carries Cecily out of the hotel to that dangling stretcher. They lay her out, head on a cushion, the rest of her stretched down wooden planks.

After she is tied securely, the PCV bends close, wishing her better luck. He promises to visit her someday in Kathmandu, then stands back and gives Beau a hard, mean stare over her broken body. Beau turns away, abruptly starting the trek. She can feel the entire village population watching them cross into lower Tala Marang and slosh up a wide trail hugging a bluff.

Later, farther on, rice fields border both sides of the trail and clouds crowd the sky. As they sway along, Cecily separates and travels above herself, watching with distant interest when the men set her down to rest and rotate. She is reminded of how Stew used to rotate the tires on his restored Studebaker back when she first met him.

Even with their burden, the porters cover twice as much ground as Cecily could have had she been totally fit. They are almost running along, knees bent. Bended knees, she notes. Bend the knees.

The group swings into Malemchi Pul in just a couple of hours for a rest and a meal. Cecily lies alone in a dim room half-full of bags of rice and fertilizer. Beau intends to sit with her, but the odor of fish emulsion drives him out.

Soon enough they are on their way. The steady bent-kneed jog of the porters lulls her until they reach Bahunepati, where the party makes a sharp right straight up one of the foothills toward Kathmandu Valley, lying south southwest.

As they make this turn away from the river and up a new trail, she is suddenly presented with a panorama of the Himalayas, unusually clear so deep into monsoon. Behind her head this whole morning was this view, this incredible chain of fangs eating half the sky. Heaving a slushy snort of awe, she spews blood clots.

Her rescue party hires a taxi at Nagarkot, paying double the meter because it is dark and again raining. They speed around Kathmandu on Ring Road and up to a hospital in Patan that is patronized by foreigners who can't get to Bangkok.

Their arrival she never remembers. She hears rumors much later of an absurd taxi ride: all four porters, Beau, and the driver crowded into an old Datsun with Cecily planked in on top.

She is also told that the doctor on duty sent Beau on to the US embassy to straighten everything out. Several hospital employees accompanied him. For once, the ambassador was speechless.

However, at the moment of Cecily's arrival, the medical staff does all the needle and tube work required to save her. On the emergency room gurney, she writhes violently and her teeth chatter. The nurses cluck their tongues in concern at her wretched condition.

Actually, the reason she writhes is because one of these nurses shoves an intravenous needle into her arm like a fork into a steak. The needle cuts through her blood vessel and lets the IV feed into her left arm, several hours passing before anyone notices. Her arm will not bend for a month, bruised indigo from wrist to armpit.

The staff changes limbs and tries again. This attempt works better, so there is no reason to suspect this more successful insertion is what gives her hepatitis before she even gets out of the hospital. Everyone blames the hepatitis on poor sanitation out in the mountains.

After all, she was out there, what? Five days? Anything could have happened.

PART V

CECILY UNBOUND

August, 1978

Antistrophe

"... nor ever may I know a heavenly wooer:
I dread such things beholding
Io's sad virginity
ravaged, ruined ..."

39

FOR TWO DAYS SHE LIES ASLEEP and unaware of the stir she has caused. No one knows the real story, which only enhances speculation. Those who had met Cecily here and there over the years, then mostly ignored her ever since, are the most outraged that such a thing could happen to someone in the diplomatic community.

Anna is her first visitor after she staggers awake. She informs a woozy Cecily that Beau is being detained at the embassy until his deportation arrangements are complete. Anna thanks her for such an entertainment to enliven monsoon: her experience, still mostly a matter of speculation, is so sensational that it's being carried like a torch from sunroom to bedroom in palaces across the valley.

Anna came the moment she learned of her friend's dramatic return. Actually, the ambassador called on Anna to ID Cecily Havenshack because that man, Beau something, wasn't talking, beyond providing his name and hers. Still in intensive care, incoherent and almost unrecognizable, Cecily could provide nothing.

On this fourth morning of hospital life, Anna returns bearing gifts. Cecily's organic narcotic state while coming down out of the mountains has been replaced by the edgy buoyancy of manufactured painkillers. She will probably be addicted when all this is over, but the pharmaceuticals leave her marooned on a high desert of detachment and she really cannot care.

She is experimenting with moving her legs and inspecting her bruised arm that won't bend when Anna sails through the door, bearing a basket piled high with books and chocolates and flowers.

As she enters, Anna wears that stunning smile that has paved her way so far through life, but today her perfect brown eyes aren't smiling along. Still, she appears all that is clean and civilized to Cecily, partly because she's wearing a tailored blue blouse and an ivory linen skirt that skims down her long legs, her sandals from Spain, sunglasses from France, the frames pushed back and holding a shiny, chin-length cut off her face, which continues clear, expected clouds in the late forties. Cecily tries to concentrate.

After Anna recovers from dismay renewed at the sight of Cecily, she informs her battered friend of Beau's detainment in the embassy's "back room." She relates how this came about because of the demands of the entire community. Even the King was heard to comment, and several of the Shahs mentioned castration at a luncheon yesterday.

Everyone assumes Beau deliberately beat her up, though there are those who ask, Why, then, didn't he just leave her out there? So, if Cecily wants Beau's manhood to remain intact, she'd better talk to the ambassador PDQ. Anna eyes her friend covertly while making this announcement.

She adds that Beau has admitted to shanghaiing Cecily from her front door Sunday morning and hauling her up to Tala Marang and back. But he keeps saying he never considered it kidnapping, exactly.

He claims he does not have a weapon, never threatened her with any weapon. Beyond that, Beau has only one thing to add: he hopes she's all right, and she's the one who had a weapon.

Cecily croaks, "That's two things."

Anna laughs hard and informs Cecily she must get well soon so she can fulfill everyone's worst expectations. Cecily relaxes at the silliness of this teasing. Surely Anna would not embark on such a droll monologue if Cecily didn't appear so well on the trek to recovery.

Anna lights a cigarette and blows smoke, completely ignoring the hospital's no smoking policy. Cecily doesn't mind. The smoke fascinates her; she observes the tendrils that curl slowly up to the ceiling. Anna takes a deep breath, exhales, plumes.

"By the way, Cecily, I thought I might need to tell you about Beau — I mean, besides him staying at the embassy."

Cecily focuses. The flexible parts of her face harden at Beau's name. Oddly hesitant, Anna speaks in a voice devoid of its normally rich tones.

"Remember the man I said I had over for dinner that night? And that he was returning the next night? I told you about him at the pool. Remember?"

Anna sits tense in her chair with one arm across her slim chest.

"Remember?" she repeats.

Cecily inclines her head more alertly.

"Well," Anna takes a ragged drag of smoke, "that was Beau."

Suddenly wide awake, Cecily stares at Anna. Did she really say that? Her fabulous date was Beau? In disbelief, Cecily croaks, "Beau?"

Anna nods. She inhales harshly, expels smoke up to the ceiling, cording her long neck. Cecily rasps out, "No! Oh, no!" Then, "Are you sure?"

"Quite sure. I saw him at the embassy. Went there on some flimflam excuse. Of course when I heard his name, it was too much of a coincidence. I mean, how many Beaus can there be in this valley at the same time? And with the same tendency to — well, it was Beau."

She inhales another drag, grimaces, leans over and stubs out her cigarette on the floor, then sits back and runs her hands up through her hair, lifting the sunglasses out and dropping them in her lap.

"And Saturday night, the night before you disappeared, he was supposed to come over again. Another dinner for two," she grimaces, "and he never showed."

She pauses, then says, "I was a little distraught about that."

She smiles wanly, her eyes filled with more misery than Cecily would have thought possible in her elegant friend.

"But I would have been even more upset if I'd known what the stupid bastard was up to."

Anna stops and takes in the ruin of Cecily Havenshack. Her face changes from woe to anger.

"As it was, I was furious at him for standing me up. Furious!" She half laughs, "I even went to that Bhairav statue, you know the one I like at Dhurbar? Well, I cursed Beau royally."

She shifts and adjusts her collar. "I can't believe this part, Cecily," she says uncomfortably, "but I even cursed you. I mean, not you, hon, in particular, I was just cursing whomever it was Beau went off with instead of me," she admits, pulling out another cigarette. She taps it on her wrist repeatedly.

"Sorry about that, really. And I'm sorry about Beau." She lights up, more smoke. "I've been wallowing in some sick form of self-pity. That is until I found out what actually happened."

Anna sighs, stares at her damaged friend. "Good luck for me, I guess. Bad luck for you." Anna waves out the match. "Should I have told you?"

"Poor Beau, such a stupid," Cecily whispers. She half smiles at Anna, continuing, "Poor us."

Anna rocks unconsciously, biting her lip. Cecily stares at her friend, her eyes dilating with a sudden thought.

"Anna?"

"What?" Anna stops rocking at Cecily's expression, repeating, "What?"

Cecily speaks carefully. "So, if I don't press charges, what, exactly, happens?"

Anna eyes her with interest. "Well, I imagine Beau would be released."

Cecily mulls this over. "Could he be deported? I mean, if I don't charge him?"

"It's possible that His Majesty's government would have some interest in doing so." Anna watches Cecily consider this information. They sit silent for a time.

Suddenly, Anna leans forward, exclaiming, "Cecily! I forgot completely! Stewart's coming home."

Cecily pops awake. "What?"

Anna continues, "He was contacted of course, when you were identified, the ambassador did it. We figured you had already been gone several days, and by the way, your household was just figuring out something wasn't right."

She makes an angry gesture, dispensing with the foolishness of employees and diplomats. Cecily is impaled by this information.

"Edna Balderwin went over to your house and found your passport and money, and your *didi* swore none of your things were gone. So they figured you must be missing, which I'd already said about ten times, and that's when the ambassador called Stewart's big boss in Washington. Then yesterday the embassy received a cable that he's started making his way back. I tell you, Cecily, there's such a big to-do going on about this, you won't believe it when you get out of here."

She believes it. Stewart would be told, of course she knew that, and obviously Stewart would be completely irate about it all. Maybe even worried? She tries to remember more about her husband, but he seems someone she knew somewhere back in her childhood.

Anna interrupts her thoughts. "And then that night Beau brought you here, and all those porters, lord! You caused a stir, Mrs. Havenshack, you really did. All of you sopping wet and filthy, and all in one taxi! Well, hard to picture. But you were a wreck, my dear, as I can attest."

Eyeing Cecily, she looks away before continuing, "So, anyhow, Stewart is on his way. Of course, his arrival depends on connections in Europe, which are always horrendous mid-summer. He has some kind of emergency clearance, of course, but Jimmy thinks it'll still be several days before he gets here, mostly because those strikes in Delhi are backing everything up in Europe."

She leans back again in the chair, duty done. Her friend will need to gather all her wits to prepare for Stewart's arrival.

Anna glances at her gold wristwatch, puts her sunglasses back on and pushes them up into her hair. She stands, saying, "They said I couldn't stay long, hon. But I'll be back as soon as they let me. I promise."

She smiles crookedly. Cecily observes Anna is deeply wounded by this whole mess, distressed at having to tell Cecily about Beau, then having to announce Stewart's pending return. Cecily has never seen her friend so flattened by anything. It is all too distressing to contemplate, she decides. Abruptly, she's too tired to concentrate.

"I brought these books, just had them lying around, so don't even take them home if you don't want to. Leave them for those expatriot junkies who come in from the bazaar for R&R. They're incredible, have you seen them? They roam up and down the halls looking very, very hungry."

Chatting, she moves around the room arranging the flowers and placing the imported chocolates within Cecily's reach, books stacked next to them. She opens a French door behind the bed for a breeze to blow away the smoke and medicinal smells. Walking back around the bed, she tugs the sheets smooth.

When she stands by Cecily's left side and looks down at her, Cecily sees the line of her friend's jaw harden. If Anna were a less dignified and self-controlled woman, she would be weeping to see all the discolored, disfigured parts of Cecily, enhanced by a distinctly yellow pallor and an appalling gauntness. Instead, she touches one finger to her friend's hair.

Anna whispers, "He was good, wasn't he?"

Cecily is startled back into clarity. The two women exchange a look without words.

But again Cecily's eyes lose their focus as drugs and exhaustion take the upper hand. Anna eyes tubes going in and out of her friend, the cast, the massive bruises, a swollen and disfigured face. The bandaged head.

She hisses, "But not *that* good."

Leaning over, she brushes Cecily's lips with her own. Her scent curls around Cecily, briefly penetrating the thickness of sleep. She barely hears the click of Anna's heels going out the door and down the corridor.

40

SO SOFT, THIS BED. This bed is her cradle, it nurtures her with umbilical cords into her arms and wrists and sinuses. This bed goes up up up. Cecily goes up too. She looks down.

Below in her hospital room her bed sits alone in the center. On it, her bony little body cuddles around a pillow. Starched white and stiff, her nightgown rubs a welt against her neck, exposed because her hair tumbles forward over the face she has hidden in the linens. For some reason she can fly best from this tortured position, and flying is such a relief.

A slight noise from the hallway just outside the door awakens her. As if it were echoing gunfire, the sound flips Cecily back into her hospital body, tense, her thoughts bouncing like balls off six hard surfaces. This disoriented moment leaves her panting. Head raised and wary, she squints at the room through blackened eyes.

Reassured that she is still alone, she creaks back flat. Heart slowing, she stares up at the ceiling, which is lovely, she thinks. Lovely how very still the ceiling is staying today.

It is also nice, she decides, not to want so much to take another pain pill. Not only not to need one so very much, but not to want to need one. That's what it is. So nice nice nice. So soft soft soft in this bed made just for her. She drifts back to sleep.

Another sound brings her half-up, her heart throbbing against her tonsils. Who — what! No one. No one? Nothing, just nothing.

She eases herself back with the starched hospital gown standing up from her chest. She sleeps lots more, and feels much better for the nourishing tea the nurses bring. They fuss and give her full drip bags and help her pee. After shooting her up with something absolutely heavenly, they leave her alone again.

41

ANOTHER DAY, MAYBE three hundred, and Cecily contentedly scratches her just-washed scalp through its still damp curls. With bandaged wrists and one little finger angled into a small metal cage, she happily clinks a spoon of sugar inside the cup of tea sitting on the bed tray. Surveying the recently scrubbed hospital room, she trills her tongue in a purr of contentment.

The hepatitis isn't developing as bad as it could have, claim the doctors. She is a lucky lady; it is turning into a mild case, after all. Yes, fortunate that she arrived when she did and is now in such excellent hands. Still, the liver damage leaves her weak.

Now when there is an unknown noise outside the door, her heart doesn't turn upside down and spill into her bowels. Now when there are unexpected sounds, she simply continues pouring tea from her darling teapot into her porcelain cup and hums a little melody while doing so.

So, it isn't until someone says, "Cecily?" that she goes quite still, actually goes catatonic for a moment.

"Stewart?" she whispers, aghast. Already? He is back already?

He stands in the doorway. Trying to control her full body reaction, Cecily carefully sets the teapot down and breathes deeply. Calmer again, having gathered courage as if pleating stiff fabric, she looks up and studies Stewart, noticing how haggard he appears, his tie loose and collar open, his suit hopelessly wilted, his hair standing on end like he's been pulling it all the way from DC.

Cecily looks back down at her bed table, picks up her napkin and touches her lips, carefully avoiding the stitches in the lower one. When she looks back up, she can face the horror on Stewart's face. The shock of her condition has left him stunned, and he sags against the door frame. But she can deal with this. She's had practice, because lots of people react like this when they walk in and see her.

Cecily ponders the tray with its half-finished tea and biscuits from England. Reluctantly, she rolls it to the side. She slowly moves her legs and swings up, sitting at last with her toes dangling above the ground.

Her husband watches her pant with the effort. When he sees her sway a bit on the edge of the bed, he leaps across the room and grabs at her to hold her upright. Her gauntness frightens him. He blanches when, this close, she looks straight at him with her panda-bear face.

"The doctors say I'll look better in a couple of months."

Stewart's eyes fill with tears. "Cecily, oh god! I, I. Oh god. My poor little girl!"

Cecily stiffens. His poor little what?

"My Cecily, my little girl, my poor poor Cecily."

Little girl? Did he say little girl? Did he say girl, actually say little girl?

She puts her palms on Stew's chest and pushes. He won't let go, hugs her tighter, so she jabs her metal cast into his Adam's apple.

He springs back. He takes in the battered nose now spread across her cheeks. When he understands her rebuff is quite serious, Stewart hugs himself, his face bent to his chest.

Cecily watches this curious behavior with interest. She blinks owlishly when Stewart finally looks up. She says, "But they say I'll never look the same."

His eyes widen, horror returning. Satisfied, she continues, "My nose. They say my nose'll never be the same. Goodbye."

He blinks, going from shock to confusion. Cecily pokes her metal finger in his chest and repeats, "Goodbye. Go away."

"Cecily!"

"I don't want to talk to you."

"Cecily!"

"I don't want to see you, either." She holds her hands over her eyes.

He says carefully, logically, "Cecily, we have to talk."

She covers her ears, eyes closed, which infuriates Stewart.

"Listen to me, damn it!"

From the doorway comes a stern voice. "Please desist immediately."

He spins to face the door. Matron strides in, accompanied by a nurse and forty years of authority. She eyes Stewart coolly.

"Mrs. Havenshack receives no visitors at this time of day."

"I'm her husband," Stewart explains through gritted teeth, adding his full name with title for some reason. Cecily thinks he sounds silly.

Matron continues, her dark gaze level. "This is not a visiting hour, Mr. Havenshack. We want no setbacks in Mrs. Havenshack's recovery."

He can think of no good response. Cecily, observing him, distantly wonders about his blood pressure.

Matron gives Cecily, who is still wavering unsteadily on the side of the high bed, an appraising glance. As she marches to Cecily's side, she edges Stewart backwards, then expertly eases her fragile patient back into a reclining position, tucking her in and ordering, "You are to rest. To rest, Mrs. Havenshack."

After smoothing back Cecily's wild curls and smiling upon her, Matron turns to the nurse. "See Mrs. Havenshack is given a sedative with lunch. Now," she turns to Stewart, "please accompany me, Mr. Havenshack, to first register as a visitor," she pauses significantly, and continues, "then we must speak about Mrs. Havenshack's medical bills."

At this information, Stewart stares blankly at Matron, then seethes as he's forced to concede. He begins to follow Matron out of the room but hesitates, glancing back at Cecily. Matron eyes him, one brow lifted, and Stewart pleads, "May I please have one minute with my wife? Just sixty lousy seconds!"

Matron halts and considers Stewart so obviously fuming while trying to appear in control. She finally takes pity on this overwrought spouse. She nods, "All right, Mr. Havenshack. Sixty seconds." Matron consults her watch.

Cecily eyes Stewart with acute dislike as he crosses back to her bed. He leans over, a seriously unhappy man.

"Now, I'm going to be right back, Cecily, because you and I have things we need to straighten out." His tension almost disables him. He searches her bruised slit-eyes for any argument.

Cecily considers him a moment, then states, "I won't be here."

"You won't be here?" He barks an unbelieving laugh and stares at Cecily's pathetic little self, repeating, "Sure, you won't be here."

"Sure, I won't," she agrees, chuckling hoarsely along.

"Well, I'll be back in a few minutes so we can work this out. You'll be gone, I suppose?"

Cecily nods, "I will."

Stewart laughs. He turns and leaves, murmuring to Matron at the door, "She says she won't be here when I return. Can you believe that? Where does she think she's going to go?" Matron does not smile.

42

STEWART TAKES ALMOST half an hour discussing and filling out paperwork with the hospital administrator. There he finds out that he, Stewart Havenshack, is personally responsible for all Cecily's medical bills. Because Mrs. Havenshack dropped all charges against Beau, the embassy refuses to pay for her, and the ambassador is furious.

Stewart almost goes ballistic when presented with the bill. Worse, he learns from Matron that Beau is already deported and long beyond Stewart's ability to wring his neck and then sue him for every dime he's ever made.

Although ordered to report immediately to the ambassador, Stewart decides it's vital to straighten out a few things with Cecily. However, Matron makes it clear that Mrs. Havenshack is really not strong enough for another visit. She adds this is especially important, seeing how Mr. Havenshack himself seems a little too tired to deal with the stress of his wife's condition.

Stewart grimly agrees, his diplomatic training in place, but Matron still escorts him all the way off the grounds. He paces idly for five minutes around the exterior wall of the hospital compound, then sneaks back through a garden gate. He walks down long halls with his hands clenched in his pockets, finally darting into Cecily's room.

She isn't there. He stares at her empty bed. He turns in a circle, one hand holding the back of his neck.

The room is definitely empty, and the French doors beyond the bed stand wide open. Stewart explodes, "Damn!" taking his hand from his neck, bringing it down and punching a fist into his other palm.

He whirls and strides to the door, then stops. Turning, he surveys the room again, something changing in his face. He shakes his head and laughs to himself, "No! No. She wouldn't?"

Stewart can't take his eyes off a closet door on the far wall. He glances briefly at the hall, then tiptoes across the room. At the closet door, he stops, smiles, softly says, "Cecily?" and knocks. Cocking his head, he asks, "You in there, Cecily?"

He jerks open the door. The closet stands quite empty. Slamming the door closed, he stands and stares at it. After a long time, he shrugs as if to kick-start himself, then crosses back to the open door of Cecily's room.

There, Stewart listens carefully before peering out into the wide hall. When the coast is clear, he exits and shuts the door behind him.

The door swings away from the wall and out into the room, and then into its frame where it clicks shut.

Cecily stands there against the wall, pressed flat behind the door all this time. The starched white gown stands out full sail from her emaciated body.

As she trembles with this effort, upright at last, Cecily's chin slowly comes up off her chest. She looks straight past her bed and out the French doors to the garden and the city and the clouded mountains beyond. A glow spreads wide across her swollen and bruised face.

Later, the nurse arrives with lunch and walks Mrs. Havenshack back to bed, tenderly helping her swallow the extra sedative Matron ordered. Cecily sleeps. She dreams she can fly.

Kathmandu, Nepal

43

THE RAINS ARE OVER. Old stone *ghats* glisten on the banks of the mighty Bagmati, now a turgid tumble of glacier melt and mica-filled runoff.

In a palace out on a western curve of Ring Road, an ornate mirror reflects farmhouses scattering to the foothills. It is early fall, the air is crisp. Mountains are clear and dominate the north sky. Fields at harvest pulse green chroma that saturates the valley in the late afternoon light.

The mirror obscures, then clears, as Cecily passes it. Out of the hospital, just back to the palace, she is packing a suitcase. Still bruised, but not so catastrophically discolored as before, she moves with purpose. Gauzy *katas* drape around her neck: they are blessings from Preema, Cook and the gardener's wife. The *katas* float as Cecily reaches, bends, turns and strides to another closet.

Since she's told no one else, not even Anna, that she's leaving, these scarves are all the blessing she's going to get. Certainly Stewart won't put one around her neck except to use it as a noose.

Stewart sits on the end of the bed. He's an unhappy man. He's trying to talk Cecily out of leaving, but she ignores him. She's been ignoring him since she woke up this morning, which drives him to sudden rage. He grabs things out of the nearest suitcase and throws them through a French window. The fabric twists and floats to the ground and sprawls on the lawn. Cecily continues packing.

Later, she rolls her stacked suitcases through the palace, room after room, hallway after hallway, across the foyer and through the three-meter front door to the far edge of the porte cochère. It is a beautiful day. Past the foothills, icy peaks lunge into the sky, frozen mid-bite. Cecily gives this spectacular horizon a thoughtful gaze; she would love to soar over those mountains, swooping up the river canyons and never ever stopping on even one white rock, ever.

The sudden whoosh and flapping of an enormous bird diving at her startles her from her reverie, causing her to knock over her suitcases as she scrambles backward, and then it is gone.

What was that? Was that actually a bird? But nothing is there. The heavens are empty and silent over the palace.

Shrugging off the incident after one more cautious inspection of the nearby sky, she restacks her luggage and begins to wheel it down the bumpy drive. Past the rose garden and past the hedge maze. Past row after row of enormous vegetables. Through the copse of fragrant trees planted by that long-dead English bride.

Stewart stands fulminating under the porte cochère, but he comes no farther. Instead, he paces. He punches air and shouts, "Where are you going?"

These four words land on the driveway around her like small bombs. Cecily pauses, considers, then replies loudly without turning around, "I'll let you know." She continues bumping her leather luggage toward the gatehouse.

Stewart strangles out, "Are you coming back?"

Cecily stops and stares ahead, blind to all but her own possible landscapes. Most of them are aerial views. When she does turn to respond, she takes in the vast and lush grounds, the crumbling palace, the spouse looking distant and stiff there at the edge of the porte cochère. She shouts, "Probably not."

Dragging her bags through the gate, Cecily looks around for a taxi. Street urchins start to descend upon the memsahib, but her bruised face and her grim look keep them at bay. They whisper to each other, eyeing her uneasily: this is a new kind of memsahib.

Spying a cab, she gestures with her chin at her luggage. The driver hops out and quickly stows it in the trunk, and they spin off toward Tribhuvan International Airport.

Past the first stretch of shops and over the Bishnumati River surging south, then along the swollen Bagmati on her right. Past the bazaar beginning up hill to her left, concrete mixing with old brick and smoke-darkened timbers, all illuminated with that end-of-monsoon glow.

Cecily can sense an energy and excitement in the city from the harvest festivals beginning this week. She'll miss the best season in the Valley, with its excess of food and brilliant music. Shrines will glisten and reek from countless sacrifices. She'll miss all those spontaneous parades. She will especially miss the two festivals of light and color.

As she watches the city roll by, her open window snags riffs of music blasting from radios, shrieking trucks bullying their way past her taxi, bicycle bells clanging everywhere and there's that loud beating of wings right outside the—what!

What? Beating of wings? Cecily is shaken; when she pales, her bruises stand out like blurred flags from every nation in the U.N. What's going on? She thinks things are getting a bit too spooky as she frantically looks out all the windows, expecting to find maybe a vulture.

Or a swan, she thinks, for some odd reason. But there is no swan in sight.

At that moment Cecily tells the driver to turn up into the bazaar. She hasn't meant to, but the urge and the need blur together. They drive deep into the bazaar; Cecily leans forward over the seat and points the way. The taxi finally winds to a stop. It can go no farther into the heart of Kathmandu, no matter what memsahib thinks.

The driver agrees to wait with her luggage. Pedestrians and bicycles squeeze by the taxi in the narrow pathway between looming old buildings and Cecily has to wait for a break in foot traffic. The driver lights a bidi and turns up the radio, its keening *raga* following her for two turns before the bazaar's sensory assault takes over.

She walks rapidly and finally comes to the entrance to the Machendranath. She ducks through the tunnel, entering its small square, ignoring deep shadows and cooing pigeons and a forest of *lingams*. Residents of the buildings around the shrine have lit lamps, creating a living tapestry of light woven into night.

But all Cecily can see is that one Greek sculpture of ancient Io on her ancient pedestal. Oil lamps around the base burn a red glow up Io's flank. Io, beleaguered and deflowered, continues forever cupping her yoni and her brow.

Cecily lifts one blessed scarf from her neck and stands on tiptoes to drape it around Io's shoulders. She swings it around twice so it drapes like Beryl Markham's and Amelia Earhardt's.

Hugging the statue in her effort, she rests her cheek against Io's marble belly, so smooth, so cool. She hugs Io with the fervor of a lover, while around her the shrine hums. With her eyes closed, Cecily's other senses memorize Kathmandu.

When Cecily finally releases Io and opens her eyes, her irises are enlarged and sharp edged. She is clear to her core. She knows exactly where she's going, and she understands exactly what she has to do to set herself on a path that will lead to the rest of this avatar. She abruptly raises her arms, stretching to the piece of sky visible just above. Hundreds of pigeons take flight from the shrine in a surge that blurs the small square.

Katas flying, Cecily strides out of Machendranath. The bazaar is raucous, but she doesn't notice. She pushes her way back through the crowds and down ever narrowing alleys to the taxi, where she squeezes in and heads to the airport and Air Nepal and due south to a date with Beau's fate.

Cecily is going to find Beau because she has to finish with him before she can be free of old debris. She needs to be free to streamline her travels and make her journeys light so nothing slows her down from here on. And that's why she's going to Calcutta: the ambassador had said Beau was deported to Calcutta from Kathmandu because that had been the next flight leaving Nepal.

And when Cecily gets to Calcutta and locates Beau, she's going to fix him good. What's more, she's going to enjoy every moment of fixing him, and then she's going to get on with her life.

That's her plan. It's a damn good plan. It's a plan that tickles her nerves. It stimulates her senses so she doesn't feel as if she's operating from the backseat of a Crown Victoria, like she used to.

Come to think of it, good old Joel is in Calcutta, too. Hey, a reunion.

Kathmandu Valley shrinks, recedes and disappears as Air Nepal passes over the last of the foothills and heads south to Calcutta. It feels so good to fly. So very right. Cecily gazes down at the vast, sunset-shadowed flatlands of northern India. The horizon is too hazy and too far away to locate, as light turns to indigo in all the heavens and on her part of earth.

GLOSSARY*

Alcmene A good and virtuous wife, Alcmene was raped by Zeus, who disguised himself as her husband. She bore Zeus's son Hercules.

Annapurnas Himalayan mountain peaks in north-central Nepal

Asan Tole important temple square (tole) in the heart of Kathmandu

avatar an incarnation or lifespan

Ayurvedic refers to Ayurveda, the ancient Hindu science of medicine

Bagmati River Kathmandu's major source of water

Bahunepati village in the Helambu region of central Nepal

Bhairav the Hindu deity Shiva in his most terrifying form

bidi a thin, often flavored cigarette made of tobacco wrapped in a tendu leaf

Bihar a state of northeast India crossed by the Ganges River; also, Buddha spent his early days in the Bihar region

Bir formal name, as in Bir Hospital

Bishnumati River early English spelling of Vishnumati River, which runs through central Kathmandu and joins the Bagmati to continue flowing south

Bistaare jaanos Please go slowly.

* English spellings commonly used in 1978

Bonsbote small village hanging off Shivapuri's northern ridge

Brahman highest Hindu caste

Brahmin Hindu priest

Budhanilkantha important village north of Kathmandu, sitting on the south slope of Shivapuri

Callisto a huntress nymph, Callisto was driven from Arcadia after being raped by Zeus, who disguised himself as the goddess Diana. Callisto was turned into a bear by Zeus's jealous wife Hera.

Chini chha It has sugar.

Chini hoina? Is it without sugar?

chiyaa tea

chokidar gatekeeper

chowk royal palace or public plaza

Danaë Imprisoned by her own father, King of Argos, Danaë was raped by Zeus, who disguised himself as a shower of gold. After Danaë bore Zeus's son Perseus, the King put the baby and her in a box and dropped them in the ocean.

Daphne Daughter of a minor river god, the nymph Daphne was hounded by Apollo. He was filled with love for her, but she wanted to die a virgin and turned into a tree to escape Apollo's lust.

Denpasar city on the island of Bali, Indonesia

dhal bhaat lentils and rice

dhobi laundry specialist

Dhurbar Square temple-lined square at heart of old Kathmandu

didi household maid

ghat riverside platform for cremation

Helambu mountain region of central Nepal

Io Daughter of a minor river god, the nymph Io was raped by Zeus, who took the form of a cloud as disguise. Zeus turned Io into a cow when he was caught by his jealous wife Hera. She doomed Io to wander the earth, plagued by a gadfly.

Jumla remote region in northwestern Nepal

juto taboo

Kali the Hindu deity of death; also, Shiva's wife in her most terrifying form

kata blessed scarf of white gauze or silk

Kathmandu capital of Nepal

Kathmandu Valley central Himalayan valley where Nepal's capital is located

Leda An important virgin nymph, Leda was raped by Zeus, who disguised himself as a swan while she bathed in a pool. One of the twins Leda bore Zeus was Helen, who caused war at Troy.

Lhasa the most sacred city of Tibetan Buddhism, famous for its inaccessibility; also, the capital of Xizang (Tibet) in southwestern PRC (People's Republic of China)

lingam a symbolic male phallus, ritually revered since prehistory

Machendranath place (nath) to worship Machendra, guardian deity of Kathmandu Valley

Mahakal village in the Helambu region of central Nepal

Ma jaane I'm going / take me.

mali gardener

Malemchi Khola river (khola) running south through the central Himalayas

Malemchi Pul village where the Malemchi Khola joins the Indrawati Khola

memsahib used in colonial India as a form of respectful address for European women; also, used today by some Hindustani speakers to address foreign women

Mithras the ancient Persian deity of light; also, a guardian against evil

momos Tibetan ravioli

naga snake

Nagarkot northeastern area of Kathmandu Valley

Nepali (pl. **Nepalis**) a native or inhabitant of Nepal; also, the Indic language of Nepal, closely related to Hindi

Newar early settlers in Kathmandu Valley who culturally impacted the rest of Asia

nirvana the extinction of self in oneness with all; the ultimate goal of Buddhist meditation

Paani china Water is gone.

Patan important city in Kathmandu Valley

Pati Bhanjyang village in the Helambu region of central Nepal

Phora Dhurbar sport and culture compound for US diplomats and other official US citizens living in Nepal

Prometheus A Titan in the Greek pantheon, Prometheus angered Zeus by sneaking fire, knowledge, language, the arts and blind hope to lowly mortals. He was chained to a rock where one of Zeus's pet birds pecked his liver out every day. It grew back each night. Zeus may have been upset because Prometheus had the gift of foresight and knew Zeus's fate and wouldn't tell him.

puja ritual offering and prayer

Punjab a region of northwest India defined by the Indus and Yamuna Rivers

Radjoot Hotel fictional hotel

raga a tonal framework for composition and improvisation, found typically in Hindic music

Raj Path highway to India; also, *Raj* refers to the historical era (1858 to 1947) when British rule and trade dominated India

Rana family name of rulers of Nepal from 1846 to 1951

Rani Pokhari Queen's Lake (pokhari)

rupee unit of Nepali money

sahib used in colonial India as a form of respectful address for European men

Saraswati the Hindu deity of learning, music and poetry; also, the wife of Brahma, a principal Hindu deity

sari a length of lightweight cloth, with one end wrapped to form a skirt and the other draped over a shoulder or the head

Shermatang village in the Helambu region of central Nepal

Sherpa traditionally Buddhist people of Tibetan descent living on the southern side of the Himalayas

Shiva a principal Hindu deity, worshiped as the destroyer and restorer of worlds, and in numerous other forms

Shivapuri Himalayan foothill (2,563 meters) marking the north side of Kathmandu Valley

swan a large, long-necked water bird that is part of several myths worldwide: in Hindu tradition, Brahma the Creator rides a swan; in Greek tradition Zeus disguises himself as a swan to rape Leda

Swayambhunath important temple complex in central Kathmandu Valley, representing the primordial Buddha

Sylvia Actually Rhea Sylvia, she was a vestal virgin surprised in sleep and raped by Mars, the son of Zeus. Sylvia bore Mars twin sons Romulus and Remus.

Tala Marang village in the Helambu region of central Nepal

tantric refers to Tantrism, a form of both Buddhism and Hinduism arising from action and direct experience; Tantrism has its origins in a Sanskrit word, tantra, which is the basic warp of threads in weaving. Therefore, tantrism is the active interweaving of spiritual and material worlds.

tarkaari vegetables

Tata Indian truck brand

Terai a narrow strip of flat land running east–west between the Himalayan foothills and the Nepal–India border

Tribhuvan former monarch of Nepal; also, name of Kathmandu's airport and university

tika a vermilion paste that Hindus apply to their foreheads, symbolizing the presence of the divine

topi close-fitting cloth hat with no brim

Yahaa roknos Stop here.

yoni a symbolic female vulva, ritually revered since prehistory

APPENDIX

Quotes from "Prometheus Bound," *Aeschylus II,* pp.138-180. Edited by David Grene and Richard Lattimore. Translated by David Grene. Chicago: University of Chicago Press, 1956.

Part I	Io	p. 163, lines 640-641
Part II	Prometheus	p. 170, lines 816-818
Part III	Prometheus	p. 161, lines 590-592
Part IV	Prometheus	p. 165, lines 718-720
Part V	Antistrophe	p. 172, lines 896-899
Part VI	Prometheus	p. 166, lines 739-740